P9-CTQ-642

HOUSEKEEPER'S
HAPPY-EVER-AFTER

HOUSEKEEPER'S HAPPY-EVER-AFTER

BY

FIONA HARPER

 MILLS & BOON

First published in Great Britain 2010
Large Print edition 2010
Harlequin Mills & Boon Limited,
Eton House, 18-24 Paradise Road,
Richmond, Surrey TW9 1SR

© Fiona Harper 2010

ISBN: 978 0 263 21227 3

Harlequin Mills & Boon policy is to use papers that are
natural, renewable and recyclable products and made
from wood grown in sustainable forests. The logging and
manufacturing process conform to the legal environmental
regulations of the country of origin.

Printed and bound in Great Britain
by CPI Antony Rowe, Chippenham, Wiltshire

For Sian and Rose,
my darling girls, who I could never, ever forget.

CHAPTER ONE

ELLIE gave in to the insistent nagging at the fringes of her sleep and woke up. She focused on the display from the digital clock next to the bed.

Two-sixteen—and she needed to go to the bathroom. But it was her first night in an unfamiliar house and she didn't really want to be crashing around in the dark, even if she was the sole occupant.

She punched her pillow and flopped onto her other side, burying her head under the duvet. She could last. Clamping her eyes shut, she shifted position again, wriggling into the mattress. The seconds sloped by in the thick silence. She lay completely still, counting her heartbeats.

Apparently she couldn't last. Bother.

She blinked and tried to see where the outline of the door was in the blackness of the bedroom. The dull green glow from the alarm clock lit the duvet but not much more. The edge of the bed was about as inviting as the edge of a cliff.

Ellie Bond, get hold of yourself! A grown woman has no business being scared of the dark. Even in the kind of huge old house that looked as if it might have ghosts or bats in the attic.

She flung the duvet off and planted her feet firmly on the carpet, but hesitated for a couple of seconds before she stood up and inched towards the wall.

Ouch! Closer than she'd guessed.

Maybe she should have paid more attention when she'd dumped her cases in here, but she'd been so exhausted she'd only managed half her unpacking before she'd fallen into the large, squashy bed.

She rubbed her shoulder and felt along the wall for the door. It was a couple of steps to the left from her point of impact. The antique handle complained as she twisted it millimetre by millimetre. She winced and opened the door slowly and carefully. Why, she didn't know. It just seemed wrong to be too noisy in someone else's house late at night, even if they were away from home.

Ellie leant out of the doorway and slid the flat of her hand along the wall in search of the light switch.

Where was the stupid thing?

Certainly not within easy reach. But as she crept along the hallway the clouds parted and sent a sliver of moonlight through the half-open curtains at the end of the landing. Bingo! She could see the bathroom door, right next to the window. She padded more speedily along the wooden floor, her bare feet sticking to the layers of old varnish.

Relief swirled through her as she scrambled inside the bathroom and yanked the light cord. A few minutes later she opened the door and froze. The moonlight had evaporated and she was left standing in the pitch-dark.

Don't panic, Ellie. Think!

There had to be logical way to deal with this.

'Okay,' she whispered out loud, 'my room is the—' she counted on her fingers '—third on the left…I think.' All she had to do was feel for the doors and she would be back in that wonderfully comfortable bed in no time.

She tiptoed close to the wood panelling, letting her left fingers walk along the surface in search of door fames.

One…

Two…

She meant to creep slowly, but with each step her pulse increased, adding speed to her steps.

Three…

She opened the door and made a quick dash for

the bed. Ever since she was a child she'd had an irrational fear that some shadowy figure underneath would grab her ankles when she got close. She'd even perfected a sprint and dive manoeuvre in her teenage years. She decided to resurrect it now.

Big mistake.

She tripped over a discarded shoe and stumbled into a solid wall of…something.

It was warm. And breathing.

Oh, heck.

There was somebody in the house! A burglar, or an axe-wielding maniac…

Her brain short-circuited. Too much information at once. Too much to process. Thankfully, more primal instincts took over. She backed away, hoping she hadn't got muddled and that the door was still directly behind her. But she hadn't made more than two steps when a large, strong hand grabbed her wrist.

Ellie's stomach somersaulted and she froze. Without even thinking about why or how, she lunged at him, whoever he was, and shoved the heel of her hand under his chin, causing him to grunt and stumble backwards.

Mother, I will never moan about the self-defence classes you made me go to in the village hall again!

In the surreal slow-motion moment that followed, she wondered why a burglar would be bare-chested in March, but before the thought was fully formed in her head his other arm grabbed her and he fell, taking her with him. She came crashing down on top of him, and then they lay winded in a tangle of arms and legs on the floor.

Here, he had the advantage. She didn't know how, but she could sense he was taller than her, and if the chest she'd just landed on was anything to go by he had five times as many muscles. Somehow as they'd fallen they'd twisted, and she was now partly pinned underneath him, her legs trapped. She started to wriggle.

I should have paid more attention at those classes, instead of gossiping at the back with Janice Bradford.

Because the man obviously had no intention of letting her loose. In one swift movement he flipped her onto her back, his hands clamping both her wrists and digging them into the scratchy wool rug while his knees clamped her thighs together. The air left Ellie's body with an 'oof' noise.

She flailed and struggled, but it was like trying to dislodge a lump of granite. Eventually she lay still beneath him, every muscle rigid. His toothpaste-scented breath came in short puffs, warming the skin of her neck. Panic fluttered in her chest.

It dawned on her that her original assumption that he was a burglar might be a tad optimistic. Things could be about to get a lot worse.

She had to act now—before he made his next move.

In a moment of pure instinct, she lifted her head and sank her teeth into the smooth skin of his shoulder. Then, while he was yelping in pain, she used every bit of strength in her five-foot-five frame to rock him to her left, getting him off-balance and thereby gaining enough momentum to swing him back in the other direction. The plan was to fling him off her so she could escape.

The plan was flawed.

He tumbled over, all right, but as she tried to crawl away he got hold of her right foot and dragged her back towards him. Ellie tried to stop herself by twisting over and clawing at the rug, but large tufts just came away in her fingers. And then she realised she was travelling further than she'd scurried away. She was being dragged back towards the bed.

That was when she started shouting. A wave of white-hot anger swept up her body.

How dared he?

'Get out of my bedroom!' she screamed. 'Or I'll—'

'What?'

He was angry, but there was something more in his voice—confusion?

Harsh light flooded the room, accompanied by the click of a switch. Ellie peeled her face off the carpet and blinked a few times, desperate to focus on anything that might give her a clue as to where the door was. Her eyes began to adjust, and she made out a tall figure against the pale blue of the wall.

Pale blue? Oh, help! My room is a kind of heritage yellow colour.

She crinkled her eyelids until they were almost shut, and swivelled her head to face her attacker. Through the blur of her eyelashes she saw a pair of deep brown eyes staring at her. There was something about them… Had she dreamt about a pair of eyes just like that before she'd woken up? Half a memory was lodged somewhere, refusing to make sense.

Ellie's chest reverberated with the pounding of her heart and she felt the fire wash up her face and settle in the tips of her ears. He looked as astonished as she felt.

She *had* seen those eyes before, but not in her

dreams. They hadn't been scowling then, but laughing, *twinkling*…

Ellie let out a noise that was part groan, part whimper as the memory clunked into place. She started to collect her limbs together and move away.

'I'm…I'm…so sorry! I got lost in the dark…' She shot a glance at him, but his face was still etched with confusion. 'I mean, I thought you were a—a maniac.'

He blinked. Something told her his assessment of her hadn't been dissimilar.

'Mr Wilder…I…'

'I know who I am. Who on earth are *you*?'

She licked her lips—they seemed to have dried out completely—and cleared her throat. 'I'm Ellie Bond, your new housekeeper.'

One month earlier

Ellie's limbs stopped working the moment she crossed the threshold of the coffee shop. The woman in the red coat was early. She wasn't supposed to be here yet, but there she was, sitting at a table and reading a newspaper. After a few seconds the door swung closed behind Ellie, hitting her on the bottom. She didn't even flinch, mainly because she felt as if she'd swallowed a thousand ice cubes and they were now all jostling for position as they slowly melted, spreading outwards through her body.

The woman's long dark hair almost touched the tabletop as she bent over an absorbing story. Chunky silver earrings glinted in her ears when she flicked her hair out of the way so she could turn the page. Earrings that Ellie had given her for her last birthday.

The woman hadn't noticed Ellie yet, and she was glad about that. She stared harder. Perhaps if she just stood here for a moment, took her time, it would come to her.

Something the woman was reading must have bothered her, because she stiffened and, even though her head was bowed, Ellie knew that three vertical lines had just appeared above the bridge of the woman's nose. That always happened when she frowned. When people had been friends for more than a decade, they tended to notice little things like that about each other without even re-alising it. The brain collected a scrapbook about a person, made up of assorted images, sensations, sounds and aromas, all of which could be called up at a moment's notice. And Ellie had plenty of those memories flooding into the front of her con-sciousness right now—untidy college bedrooms, the smell of dusty books in the library, the giggles of late-night gossip sessions…

A fact that only made the current situation more galling.

Ellie couldn't remember her name.

Since the accident, finding the right name or word had become like rummaging around in the cupboard under the stairs without a torch. She knew the information she wanted was in her brain somewhere, but she was fumbling in the dark, not really knowing what she was looking for and just hoping she'd recognise it when she finally laid hold of it.

A waitress bustled past her, and the movement must have alerted her friend to the person standing at the edge of her peripheral vision, because she looked up from her newspaper and smiled at Ellie.

Ellie waved back, but behind her answering smile she was running through the letters of the alphabet, just as she'd been taught at the support group, to see if any of them jogged her memory.

Anna? Alice? Amy?

The woman stood up, beaming now, and Ellie had no choice but to start walking towards her.

Belinda? No.

Brenda?

The chunky earrings bobbed as her friend stood and drew her into a hug. Ellie just stood there for a moment like a rag doll, and then she made a conscious decision to contract her arm muscles and squeeze back. Not that she was opposed to hugging; it was just that her brain was far too busy ferreting around for the right letter, the right syllable, to get her started.

Christine...Caroline...Carly?

Carly. It seemed right and not right at the same time.

A whisper tickled her ear. 'It's so good to see you, Ellie!'

Ellie knew her friend would understand if she just admitted her memory blank. But Ellie was fed up with being *understood*. She just wanted to *be*— to live her life the way everyone else did, without the sympathetic glances. That was why she'd arranged this meeting in the first place.

A familiar sensation washed over her. She imagined it to be what it might feel like if portions of her memory were buoys, chained to a deep and murky ocean floor, and then all of a sudden one freed itself and floated upwards, arriving on the surface with a plop.

Charlotte Maxwell.

'Hi, Charlie,' she said, and finally relaxed into the hug. 'It's good to see you too.'

She tried not to, but as she pulled away and sat down Ellie sighed, deep and hard. Charlie tilted her head and looked at her.

'How are you?'

Ah. How innocent that phrase sounded. How kind and well-meaning.

Ellie had come to hate it. People were always asking her that, normally wearing a concerned expression. Oh, she wasn't fooled a bit. It wasn't small talk. Chit-chat. What people wanted from her when they asked that question was a full psychological and medical rundown.

She smiled, but her lips remained firmly pressed together. 'I'm great. Really.'

Charlie kept staring at her. 'Still getting the headaches?'

'Only occasionally,' she replied, shrugging the observation away.

The wicked twinkle returned to Charlie's eyes as she stood back and looked Ellie up and down. 'You've had your hair cut,' she said.

Ellie automatically raised a hand to feel the blunt ends of her tousled blonde curls. She'd only had it done a few days ago, and she still wasn't used to finding fresh air where there had once been heavy ringlets that reached halfway down her back. The ends now just brushed the tops of her shoulders. It was shorter, maybe a bit younger, and a heck of a lot more manageable.

'I was ready for a change,' she said.

Change.

That was why she was here. She might as well get down to business and ask Charlie the question that had been burning her tongue all morning. If she didn't do it soon she was likely to get distracted and end up going home without mentioning it at all. She opened her mouth to speak.

'I don't know about you,' Charlie said in a grave voice, 'but I can't be expected to indulge in a month's worth of gossip without a side order of caffeine—and possibly a muffin or three. It's just not done.'

Ellie glanced over at the counter then stood up. 'I'll have a…'

Oh, flip. What was the word? She knew she knew it, but it seemed to be speeding away from her, like a dream that was fast evaporating with the last traces of sleep.

'You know…the fluffy, milky drink with powder on top.'

Charlie didn't bat an eyelid, bless her. 'Two cappuccinos, please,' she said to the barista.

Ellie leaned forward and looked at the girl over Charlie's shoulder. 'And a chocolate muffin, please.'

'Make that two.' Charlie turned and smirked at her while the barista rang up the sale. 'That's my girl. Couldn't forget chocolate if you tried.'

If her mother or her sister had said something like that Ellie would have snapped at them, but she found herself laughing at Charlie's sideways comment. Maybe she was too sensitive these days. And she'd wound herself up into a state about meeting Charlie before she'd even got here. No wonder her memory was malfunctioning. It always got worse when she was stressed or nervous.

Charlie understood. She made Ellie's 'condition' seem like no big deal. That one positive thought gave her confidence. She was going to ask her. She was ready.

But the first cappuccinos had been drained and the second round ordered before Ellie finally worked up her nerve. She twiddled the silver locket she always wore between her thumb and forefinger.

'Actually, Charlie, there was a reason I suggested getting together this morning. I need a favour.'

'Anything. You know that.' Charlie leaned forward and rubbed her forearm. 'I'll do anything I can to help.'

Ellie took at deep breath. She was asking for a lot more than the usual sympathetic ear or moral support at social functions. A lot more.

'I need a job.'

Charlie just seemed to freeze. She blinked a couple of times. 'A job?'

Ellie squeezed her bottom lip between her teeth and gave a little nod, but Charlie broke eye contact and took her time while she folded a corner of the newspaper page into a neat triangle. She glanced up once she'd scored it with a long, red fingernail.

'I'm sorry, Ellie. I only need a couple of people in the office, and I've got all the staff I require at the moment.'

Oh, fab. Charlie thought she was asking her for a pity job—one with minimum responsibilities and no challenges. But Ellie couldn't give up now. She was desperate. She stopped fiddling with her locket and folded her hands in her lap.

'No. I mean I want you to put me on your agency's books, preferably for a job where I can live in. I need to…get away from Barkleigh for a while. You must have something I could do?

Something that uses my skills? You know I'm a fantastic cook.'

Charlie nodded and said nothing, but Ellie could see her mind working. She made a rather nice living running an exclusive little agency providing the well-off with domestic staff—from butlers and chauffeurs to cooks and nannies.

'But are you…? Can you…?' Charlie wrinkled her nose and paused.

Ellie knew what she was trying to ask, what she really didn't want to put into words. Was the patched-up and rehabilitated Ellie capable of holding down a full-time job? The truth was, Ellie wasn't even sure herself. She thought she was. She'd worked hard to put strategies and coping mechanisms in place to help with the memory and concentration problems that were so common after a serious head injury, but she was shaking in her boots at the idea of moving away from everything familiar and starting again somewhere new.

'I just have to work a little bit harder than everyone else at keeping myself organised nowadays. But I can do this, Charlie. I know I can. I just need someone to believe in me and give me a chance, and you said you'd do anything you can to help.'

Okay, that was playing dirty, but she was desperate. The pained look on Charlie's face was almost too much to bear. She wasn't convinced. And if Ellie had been in her shoes maybe she wouldn't have been either.

For a long time Charlie said nothing, and Ellie thought she might be creating brand-new wrinkles on her forehead with all the mental wrestling she was doing. Then, slowly, the lines faded.

'Okay,' she said, staring out of the window. 'I just might have something. I'll let you know.'

The cottage door slammed. There was something very final about the sound of the old door hitting the door frame. Ellie tried to remove the key from the worn Victorian lock, but it refused to budge.

Today was not going well. Lost keys, a case that wouldn't shut and a pigeon stuck in the roof had already plagued her this morning. If she had been one to believe in bad omens she'd have run upstairs and hidden under her duvet a few hours ago. But the duvet was freshly laundered, waiting for someone else, and the rest of her life had been divided into packing boxes and suitcases. The cottage was now bare of all personal possessions, ready to be rented out by the week. The holiday lettings company had jumped at the chance of a child-friendly property in the picturesque little village of Barkleigh. Other families would build memories here now.

She caught the tip of her tongue between her teeth and resumed her negotiations with the lock. The choreographed sequence of turns, pulls and twists had long ago become a matter of muscle memory rather than conscious thought, and finally the key jerked free. It always did in the end. It just needed a little gentle persuasion.

It was time to leave. Ellie shoved her keys in the back pocket of her jeans and stared through the stained glass panels that filled the top half of the heavy old door. Once, the hallway had been warm and inviting, filled with discarded shoes, coats hanging haphazardly on a row of hooks. Now it was cold and empty, distorted through the rippling glass.

A large drop of rain splashed onto the top of her head. She shuddered, picked up the last piece of luggage, then turned and walked down the path towards her waiting car.

Ellie looked out across the fields. An overstuffed dark grey cloud was devouring the sunshine, heading straight towards her. Another plop of rain dropped on the back of her neck and ran down between her shoulder blades. She increased her speed. The boot of her old hatchback stood gaping and she slung the holdall in the back, slammed the door shut and hurried round to the driver's door. The tempo of the rain increased. By the time she was inside it was drumming an unpromising rhythm on the roof of the car. Warm, earthy smells drifted through the ventilation system.

She glanced at the handbag sitting on the passenger seat. Poking out of the top was a worn blue teddy bear with one eye and bald ears where the fluff had been loved off. The backs of her eyes burned, but she refused to blink, knowing that any moisture leaking over her lashes would feel like acid. The pummelling on the roof of the car magnified, filling her ears and pulling the world away from her down a long, invisible tunnel.

Not now. Today of all days I need to keep it together.

She forced herself to sit upright in the driver's seat and stared blindly into the blurry grey scenery beyond the windscreen, then turned the key in the ignition. The car rumbled grudgingly to life, coughed once, and promptly stalled.

Still she didn't blink, just held her breath for a few seconds, then reached out to stroke the dashboard.

Come on, girl! Don't let me down now.

She pumped the gas a few times and tried again, and when the engine rewarded her with an uneven purr, she released her breath and put the car into gear. She pulled away slowly, rumbling down the country lane, and didn't allow herself the luxury of looking back.

An hour later she was sitting behind a caravan on the motorway. It was only going at about fifty, but she made no attempt to pass it. This speed was fine, thank you very much. Driving wasn't her favourite occupation these days, and she hadn't been on a motorway in a long time. She distracted herself from the haulage trucks passing her at insane speeds with thoughts of fresh starts and new jobs.

Everyone had been so happy when she'd come out of hospital after the accident, sure she was going to be 'back to normal' in no time. And after a year, when she'd finally moved out of her parents' house and back into the cottage, her family and friends had breathed a collective sigh of relief.

That was it. Everything done and dusted. Ellie is all better and we can stop worrying now.

But Ellie wasn't all better. Her hair might have grown again and covered the uneven scars on her skull, she might even talk and walk the same, but nothing, *nothing*, would ever be the same again. Underneath the 'normal' surface she was fundamentally different and always would be.

She focused on the droplets of rain collecting on the windscreen.

Water. That was all those tiny splashes were. Almost nothing, really. So how could something so inconsequential alter the course of three lives so totally, so drastically? She nudged the lever next to the steering wheel again and the specks of water vanished in a flurry of motion.

Thankfully, within a few minutes the rain had stopped completely and she was able to slow the squeaking wipers to a halt. Warm afternoon light cut clean paths through the clouds. Her shoulder blades eased back into their normal position and she realised she'd been clenching her teeth from the moment she'd put her foot on the accelerator. She made a conscious effort to relax her jaw and stretched her fingers. The knuckles creaked, stiff from gripping the steering wheel just a little too tightly.

A big blue sign was up ahead and she read it carefully.

Junction Eight. Two more to go.

She'd promised herself that she would not zone

out and sail past the turn-off. Getting lost was not an option today.

The caravan in front slowed until it was practically crawling along. Ellie glanced in her wing mirror. She could overtake it if she wanted to. The adjacent lane was almost clear. Still, it took her five minutes and a stiff lecture before she signalled and pulled out.

She was still concentrating on remembering to exit at Junction Ten, visualising the number, burning it onto her short-term memory, when a prolonged horn blast startled her. A car loomed large in her rear-view mirror. It inched closer, until their bumpers were almost touching, its engine snarling. Ellie was almost frightened enough to speed up to give herself breathing room. Almost.

Flustered, she grabbed at the levers round the steering wheel for the indicator, only to discover she'd turned the fog light on instead. She fought to keep her breathing calm, yanked at the correct lever and pulled into the inside lane. What she now realised was a sleek Porsche zoomed past in a bright red blur.

A sigh of relief was halfway across her lips when the same car swerved in front of her. She stamped on the brake and glared at the disappearing number plate, retaliating by pressing her thumb on the horn for a good five seconds, even though the lunatic driver was now a speck in the distance, too far away to hear—or care.

It had to be a man. Too caught up in his own ego to think about anyone else. Pathetic. She had made a policy to keep her distance from that type of person, whether he was inside a low-slung car or out of it.

She shook her head and returned her concentration to the road, relieved to see she was only two miles from the next service station. An impromptu caffeine break was in order.

It wasn't long before she was out of the car and sitting in an uncomfortable plastic seat with a grimy mug of coffee on the table in front of her. She cupped her hands round it and let the heat warm her palms.

The crazy Porsche driver had flustered her, brought back feelings and memories she had long tried to evade. Which on the surface seemed odd, because she couldn't even remember the accident itself.

But perhaps it was better not to have been conscious as they'd cut her from the wreckage of the family car, the bodies of her husband and daughter beside her. Not that her battered memory didn't invent images and torture her with them in the depths of the night.

She had no clear memories of the beginning of her hospital stay either. The doctors had told her this was normal. Post-traumatic amnesia. When she tried to think back to that time it was as if a cloud had settled over it, thick and impenetrable.

Sometimes she thought it would be nice to lose herself in that fog again, because emerging from it, scarred and confused, to find her lovely Sam and her darling eight-year-old Chloe were gone for ever had been the single worst moment of her existence.

All because it had rained. And because two boys in a fast car hadn't thought that important. They'd been arrogant, thinking those little drops of *almost nothing* couldn't stop them, couldn't spoil their fun.

She looked down at her coffee. The cup was empty, but she didn't remember drinking it.

Just as well.

Brown scum had settled at the bottom of the cup. Ellie shook off a shudder and patted down her unruly blonde curls, tucking the ends of the long fringe behind her ears. She couldn't sit here all day nursing an empty cup of coffee. But moving meant getting back in the car and rejoining the motorway.

Something she wanted to do even less now than she had when she'd left home this morning. She closed her eyes and slowly inflated her lungs.

Come on, Ellie. The only other option is admitting defeat and going back home to hibernate for ever. You can do this. You have to. Staying at the cottage is eating you alive from the inside out. You're stagnating.

She opened her eyelids, smoothed her T-shirt down over her jeans, swung her handbag out from underneath the table and made a straight line for the exit.

Back on the road, her geriatric car protested as she reached the speed limit. She filtered out the rattling and let the solitude of the motorway envelop her. She wasn't thinking of anything in particular, but she wasn't giving her attention to the road either. Her mind was in limbo—and it was wonderful.

The sun emerged from the melting clouds and flickered through the tops of the trees. She flipped the visor down to shield her eyes. The slanting light reflected off the sodden carriageway and she peered hard at the road, struggling to see the white lines marking the lanes.

In fact, she was concentrating so hard she failed

to notice the motorway sign on the grassy verge to her left.

Junction Ten.

CHAPTER TWO

WHEN she finally arrived, her new workplace was a bit of a surprise. Big shots like her new boss normally wanted their homes to shout out loud how rich and grand their owners were. Yet as she drove up the sweeping gravel drive and the woodland parted to reveal Larkford Place, she discovered a small but charming sixteenth-century manor house surrounded by rhododendrons and twisting oaks. The mellow red bricks were tinted gold by the rays of the setting sun, and the scent of lavender was thick in the air after the rain. The house was so much a part of its surroundings she could almost imagine it had grown up together with the ancient wisteria that clung to its walls.

For the first time since she'd decided to escape from her life she felt something other than fear or desperation. It was beautiful here. So serene. Hope surged through her—an emotion she hadn't experienced in such a long time that she'd assumed it must have been wiped clear of her damaged memory banks with everything else.

The drive swelled and widened in front of the house, a perfect place to park cars. But this wasn't where she was stopping—oh, no. It was the lowly tradesmen's entrance for her. She changed gear and followed a narrower branch of the drive round the side of the house and into a cobbled courtyard. The old stables still had large glossy black doors, and Ellie admired the wrought-iron saddle rest that was bolted to the wall as she got out of her car and gave her legs a stretch.

Once out of the car, she stood motionless in the courtyard and stared at the ivy framing the back door. Wind rippled through it, making it shiver. With measured steps she approached it, pulling the key she'd picked up from the previous house-keeper out of her pocket, then sliding it into the old iron lock. She pushed the wooden door open and peered down a dark corridor.

The excitement she'd felt only moments ago drained away rapidly, gurgling in her stomach as it went. This threshold was where yesterday and tomorrow intersected. Crossing it felt final, as if by taking that step other doors in her life would slam shut and there would be no return.

But that was what she wanted, wasn't it? To move forward? To leave the past behind?

She willed her right leg to swing forward and make the first step, and once she'd got that over with she marched herself down the corridor, her footsteps loud and squeaky on the flagstones, announcing her decision and scaring any ghosts away.

A door led to a bright spacious kitchen, with a pretty view of the garden through pair of French windows on the opposite side of the room.

Ellie turned on her heels and took a better look at the place that would be her domain from now on. It was a cook's dream. The house had been newly renovated, and she'd been told the kitchen fitters had only finished last week. The appliances looked as if they'd walked straight out of a high-end catalogue. They even smelled new.

A long shelf along one wall held a row of pristine cookery books. She wandered over to them as if suddenly magnetised. *Ooh.* She'd been eyeing this one in her local bookshop only last week…

Without checking her impulse, she hooked a finger on the top of the binding and eased it off the shelf. She had plenty of time to explore the house—almost a whole week—before her new boss arrived home from his overseas trip. The wall planner and the sticky notes could come out tomorrow, when her brain was in better shape to make sense of all these unfamiliar sights and sounds. Right now she needed to rest. It had been a long and tiring day and she deserved a cup of tea and a sit-down. She opened the book and flicked a few pages. It was legitimate research, after all…

It didn't take long to locate the kettle, the teabags and even a packet of chocolate digestives. While she waited for the water to boil she wandered round the kitchen, inspecting it more closely. What was that under the wall cabinet? It looked like a…

Oh, cool. A little flatscreen TV that flipped down and swivelled in any direction you wanted. She pressed the button on the side and a crisp, bright picture filled the screen—a teatime quiz show. She'd work out how to change channels later. For now it was just nice to have some colourful company in the empty house, even if the acid-voiced presenter was getting rather personal about a contestant who wasn't doing very well.

She made her tea and hoisted herself onto one of the stools at the breakfast bar, the cookery book laid flat in front of her, and started dunking biscuits into her mug before sucking the chocolate off. Nobody was here to catch her, were they?

Now, what could she cook Mr Big Shot for dinner on his first night back? It had to be something impressive, something to make him want to hire her permanently when the three-month trial period was up.

Ellie suspected she wouldn't have been offered the job if the man in question hadn't been a) Charlie's cousin and b) desperate for someone to start as soon as possible. Her new boss was something big in the music industry, apparently. She thought the name had sounded vaguely familiar, but she really didn't keep up to date with that sort of thing any more.

Her oldest friend, Ginny, had actually seemed impressed when Ellie had made the announcement about her new job. She'd gushed and twittered and gone on about how lucky Ellie was. Ellie hadn't stopped her, glad that Ginny had been too distracted to ask any difficult questions about the *real* reason for Ellie's sudden need to uproot herself from her comfortable little life and flee.

But she wasn't going to think about that at the moment. For once she was grateful for her brain's tendency to flit onto a new subject without a backward glance, and turned her whole attention to the colourful book on the counter in front of her.

Now, was squid-ink pasta really as stupendous as those TV chefs made out? Or did they just use it because it made the pictures in their glossy cookbooks look good?

The cooking part of the job would be fun. She'd always enjoyed it, and had even taken a few courses at the local adult education college to hone her techniques before Chloe had been born. In the last couple of years it had become almost an obsession. But obsessions were something she could excel in these days, and since she'd been out of the workforce and had a lot of time on her hands it had been a perfect way to keep herself occupied. Funnily, it was the one skill she seemed to have clung on to without any deficit since the accident. She didn't know why. Perhaps that knack of combining flavours and textures was held in a different part of the brain—one that hadn't been shaken and swollen and bruised as the car had rolled and crumpled around her.

There it was again, that feeling that the world was retreating, leaving her in an echoey bubble all on her own. Her fingers automatically found her locket while she tried to distract herself with the book. Initially the print blurred and the pictures refused to stay in focus, but she blinked twice and forced her eyes to work in unison, and eventually everything slid back to normal.

The television was still on low in the background and Ellie glanced at it. The quiz show she'd had half an ear on was over and something else had started. It looked like some red carpet thing that was obviously going to clog up the TV schedule for the rest of the evening. An eager reporter in a low-cut top clutched her microphone and tried not to let on she was shivering in the brisk March wind.

Just then a graphic flashed up at the bottom of the screen. Ellie did a double-take, then lurched forward in an effort to get closer to the television—anything to help her unscramble the images swarming up her optic nerve and into her brain.

'That's—that's him!'

The book lay on the counter, forgotten, and her finger, which had been scanning a list of ingredients, now hovered uselessly in mid-air. She jumped off the stool, walked over to the little TV and used that very same finger to drum on the volume button.

'*Mark Wilder*', the caption at the bottom of the screen said.

Her new boss.

Crumbs, she could see why Ginny had gone all twittery now. He certainly was very good-looking, all ruffled dark hair and perfect teeth. Not that those things really mattered when it came down to forging a long-lasting relationship. Nice dental work amounted to nothing if the man in question turned out to be a shallow, self-centred waste of space. She was much more interested in what a man was like on the inside.

She looked at Mark Wilder again, *really* looked at him. He was about the same age as her. Mid-thirties? Possibly older if he was aging well—and, let's face it, his sort usually did. But who was he beneath the crisp white shirt and the designer suit? More importantly, what would he be like to work for? She stood, hands on hips, and frowned a little. When Charlie had phoned to offer this position she'd been too excited that her plan was coming to fruition to think much about her future employer. He'd been more of an escape route than a person, really.

Suddenly a woman slid into shot beside him—early twenties, gravity-defying bust and attire that, if it stretched in the wash, might *just* qualify as a dress.

Ellie sighed.

Oh, he was *that* kind of man. How disappointing.

The reporter in the cleavage-revealing top didn't seem to be bothered, though. She lurched at him from behind the metal barrier. 'Mr Wilder! Melissa Morgan from Channel Six!'

Oh, yes. That was her name.

This should be interesting. From what Ellie remembered, this woman had a reputation for asking awkward questions, being a little bit sassy with her interviewees. It made for great celebrity sound-bites. You never knew what juicy little secrets she might get her victims to accidentally reveal.

Wilder spotted the reporter and strode over to her, his movements lean and easy. In the crowd, a couple of hundred pairs of female eyes swivelled to track his progress. Except, ironically, those of his girlfriend. She was looking straight at the camera lens.

Even the normally cool reporter was fawning all over him. Not that Wilder seemed to mind. His eyes held a mischievous twinkle as he waited for her to ask her question.

'Pull yourself together, woman!' Ellie mumbled as she brushed biscuit crumbs off the cookery book with the side of her hand.

Melissa Morgan blushed and asked her question

in a husky voice. 'Are you confident your newest client, Kat De Souza, will be picking up the award for best female newcomer this evening?'

Go on, Ellie silently urged. Prove me wrong. Be charming and gracious and modest.

He increased the wattage on his smile. The reporter looked as if she was about to melt into a puddle of pure hormones.

'I have every confidence in Kat,' he said in a warm, deep voice, appearing desperately serious. But then his eyes did that twinkly thing again. 'Of course, having superior management doesn't hurt.'

How did he do that? Special eye drops?

Of course the reporter fell for it. She practically tripped over her own tongue as she asked the next question. Wilder, in turn, lapped up the attention, deliberately flirting with her—well, maybe not flirting, exactly, but he had to be doing *something* to make her go all giggly like that.

Ellie reached for another digestive without taking her eyes off the television, and knocked the packet onto the floor. The man seemed to be enjoying the fact that a couple of million viewers were catching every second of his very public ego massage. And what was even more annoying was that he batted each of the reporter's questions away with effortless charm, never losing his cool for an instant.

There was no end to the reporter's gushing. 'I'm sure you are not surprised to discover that, due to your success as one of the top managers in the recording industry today, *Gloss!* magazine has named you their most eligible bachelor in their annual list.'

He clasped his hand to his chest in mock surprise. 'What? *Again!*'

Oh, great. Self-deprecating as well as shy and retiring. This guy was going to be a blast to work for. Just as well Charlie had said he spent the greater part of the year travelling or in endless meetings.

He stopped smiling and looked deep into the reporter's eyes. 'Well, somebody had better just hurry up and marry me, then.' He looked around the crowd. The grin made an encore. 'Anyone interested?'

The reporter blushed and stuttered. Was it just Ellie's imagination, or was she actually considering vaulting the barrier? And Ellie didn't think she was the only one. Something about the scene reminded her of a Sunday night nature programme she'd seen recently—one about wildebeest. A stampede at this moment was almost inevitable.

She flapped her book closed, ignoring the puff of crumbs that flew into the air, and let out a snort.

The reporter stopped simpering and suddenly smoothed her hair down with her free hand. Her spine straightened. About time too, Ellie thought. This woman was supposed to be a professional. How embarrassing to catch yourself acting like that on national television.

This time when she fired her question, the reporter's voice was cool and slow. 'Was it hard to rebuild your career after such...*difficult* beginnings, both in your professional and personal life?'

Her face was a picture of sympathy, but the eyes glittered with a hint of ice. Ellie almost felt a tremor of sympathy for him. But not quite.

Something other than lazy good humour flashed in Mark Wilder's eyes.

'Thanks for the good wishes.' He paused as his stare hardened and turned to granite. 'Good evening, Ms Morgan.' And then he just turned and walked away.

The reporter's jaw slackened. It was as if she'd been freeze-framed by her own personal remote control and all she could do was watch him stride away. The camera shook a little, then panned to include Mr Wilder's companion. Miss Silicone pouted a smile and trotted after her man, leaving the floundering reporter to find another celebrity to fill the gaping space in front of her microphone. She turned back to the cameraman, looking more than a little desperate, and then the picture cut to a long shot of the red carpet.

Ellie shook her head, punched the button on the side of the TV and flapped it back into place under the cabinet. She was starting to fear that this whole new job idea was one of the random impulses that had plagued her since the accident—just another one of her brain's little jokes.

She tucked the cookery book under her arm and tossed the empty biscuit packet in the direction of the bin. It missed.

With a few long strides Mark put as much distance as he could between himself and the trouble his smart mouth had caused him. Flashguns zapped at him from every direction. Suddenly his expensive suit seemed really flimsy. No protection at all, really.

He'd been bored enough to welcome the devilish urge to tease Melissa Morgan, but he'd forgotten that behind the batting eyelashes was an intelligent reporter—one who didn't hesitate to go for the jugular where a morsel of celebrity gossip was concerned. She'd done a number on quite a few of his firm's clients in recent years, and the opportunity for a little payback had just been too tempting. But it had backfired on him, hadn't it? The story he'd wanted her to focus on tonight was Kat and her award nomination, not his own less-than-glorious past.

He glanced at the crowd bulging against the barriers as he overtook an up-and-coming British actress in a long, flowing gown. He should be loving every second of this. It was the life he'd always worked for. What most people sitting in front of their TVs with their dinners on their laps dreamed of—red carpets, beautiful women, fast cars, exotic locations, more cash than they knew what to do with…

So what was wrong with him?

He shook his head to clear the baying of the photographers, the screaming of the crowd, and became aware of determined footsteps behind him.

Oh, heck. Melodie. Ms Morgan must have got him more rattled than he'd thought. He gave himself a mental slap for his lack of chivalry and turned and waited for her. She was only a few paces behind him, and as she came level with him he placed a guiding hand on her elbow.

Melodie's agent had called his PA a couple of weeks ago and asked if he would like to meet her. This was what the love lives of the rich and famous had come to. Relationships were practically conducted in the third person. *My people will call your people...*

He didn't normally respond to requests like this, but he'd needed a date tonight at short notice, and Melodie was young, sexy and stunning—just the sort of woman he was expected to have on his arm at a bash like this. It didn't matter that he suspected she didn't have any romantic yearnings for him when he'd called to ask her out. And that the industry grapevine had confirmed that a certain C-list model was looking to kick-start a pop career.

It was all very predictable. But predictable was good. At least he knew what to expect from this self-serving approach, even if his choice in female companions only inflamed the tabloid gossip about his private life. He hadn't even met half the women the papers had paired him with. And the ones he did date were just like the woman walking next to him: happy to use him for their own ends.

Good for them. It was a dog-eat-dog world and he'd learned one vital piece of wisdom early on: the woman who talked of love and commitment was the one who turned and bit you on the butt when you were least expecting it. He had the scars to prove it.

They moved inside the old theatre. Had they redone the décor in here? It had seemed opulent and elegant last time he was here, but now the crimson walls screamed at him, and the gold leaf everywhere just hurt his eyes.

He hadn't planned on coming to the awards this evening, but duty had called. Or, to be more accurate, duty had cried and pleaded down the phone in the shape of his newest and youngest signing, Kat De Souza.

They reached a flight of stairs and he held back and let Melodie walk up the sweeping staircase in front of him. Her dress was shimmering silver, backless, with a neckline slashed almost to her navel. It clung in all the right places. And Melodie certainly had *places*. Mark did his best to appreciate the view, but his pulse was alarmingly regular. Just another indicator that he was out of sorts tonight. Must be the jet lag.

An usher led them to their table at the front of the auditorium. Kat was already there, with her boyfriend *du jour*. This one was a drummer, or something like that. Mark pulled out Melodie's chair for her and made the introductions, then leaned across to Kat.

'Nervous?'

Her head bobbed in small, rapid movements.

'Sorry I woke you up and snivelled down the phone at you the other day.' She paused to twirl one of her long dark ringlets around a finger with a bitten-down nail before looking up at him again. 'The time differences are so confusing, and I was in a bit of a state.'

He remembered. Technically, although he'd been the one to 'discover' Kat, after he'd walked past her busking on the Underground, he wasn't her personal manager. He was careful not to get too close to his clients nowadays, normally leaving the legwork to his junior associates. He'd been in the business long enough to pay his dues, and had ridden more tour buses and slept on more recording studio floors during all-night recording sessions than he cared to remember. He'd paired Kat up with Sasha, a hip, energetic young woman at his firm who had the potential to go far. But where he'd hoped there would be female bonding, there had only been friction.

In the end he'd decided to step in and take an active interest for a few months—ease the teething process, if you like. Kat was only seventeen, and a bit overwhelmed at her sudden shove into the spotlight. She needed stability at the moment, not constant bickering. A happy client was a productive client, after all.

Mark smiled back at Kat and waited for her to finish fidgeting with her hair. 'Who needs sleep, anyway?' he said, giving her a little wink.

'I'm so grateful you changed your plans and flew in at the last minute. I'm frantic! I don't know whether I'm more scared of winning or not winning. How crazy is that? And I reckon I need all the support I can get.'

The scruffy excuse for a musician sitting next to her swigged a mouthful of champagne out of the bottle and produced a proud burp. Mark shifted position and tried to block his view of him with the avant-garde floral arrangement exploding from the centre of the table.

Great choice of support, Kat. First class.

Proof, yet again, that his client was young and naive and definitely needed a guiding hand.

With the uncanny knack females had of confirming his opinions of them, Kat reached for the glass of champagne in front of her and swung it towards her lips. Mark's arm shot out in a reflex action that stopped the flute reaching its destination.

'Hey!'

He prised the glass from her fingers. 'No, you don't, young lady! You're underage.'

Kat's chin jutted forward as she had one of her teenage Jekyll and Hyde moments, switching from sweet and grateful to sour and belligerent in the snap of a finger. 'Chill out, Mark! You can't tell me what to do, anyway. You only manage my career, not my personal life.'

Okay, technically she was right. And if it had been anyone else on his agency's books he would have minded his own business. But it just didn't seem right to sit there and do nothing.

'No, you're right. I can't tell you what to do, but I can *advise* you. It's my job to look after your best interests. It's what I take my fifteen percent for, after all.' He placed the glass out of reach behind the spiky centrepiece. 'Anyway, you don't want to be tipsy when you collect the award later. And I mean *when*, not *if*.'

When in doubt, flatter. It always worked. He raised his eyebrows and waited for the thaw.

Kat's blistering stare softened a fraction. Girls of her age could be fiendishly stubborn. It was just as well he seemed to have the knack of charming each and every female he met, whether they were nine or ninety. Kat continued to glower at him, but he knew he'd won. He would let her back down gracefully without pressing the point further.

'Water is better for my voice, anyway,' she said, lounging back on her revolting boyfriend to give him a defiant kiss.

Mark beckoned a waiter and smiled to himself while his face was hidden.

Six months ago no one had heard of Kat De Souza. Despite her youth, she had a wonderfully mature soulful voice. Not only that, but she wrote the most amazing love songs and played the acoustic guitar to accompany herself. Her pared-down debut single had been a smash hit, catapulting her to overnight fame. His firm's expertise and connections had helped, of course, but she had ten times the talent of some of his other clients. Securing a recording deal had been a breeze. Now he just had to make sure that the pressure and the insanity of the music industry didn't derail her before she got to where she was destined to go.

He watched Kat bite her thumbnail down to a level that surely had to be painful. Mature talent, sure, but she was still just a scared schoolgirl underneath all the bluster. He was glad he'd shuffled his life around to be here tonight.

At that moment a wave of unexpected tiredness rolled over him. He hid a yawn and ignored the jet lag pulling at his eyelids.

It was going to be a long night.

Once Ellie had rustled herself up something more filling than biscuits to eat from the well-stocked larder, she decided to give herself a tour of Larkford Place. Tomorrow she'd get her Post-it notes out and label every door in the house—which was saying something. It seemed as if there were hundreds of them, all leading to rooms and corridors you wouldn't expect them to.

The scraps of coloured paper would be gone again by the time her boss returned, of course. It wasn't everybody's taste in décor. But in the meantime they'd help her to create some new neural pathways, remember the layout of the house. So, hopefully, when she wanted to cook something she'd end up in the kitchen and not the broom cupboard. She'd had to resort to this technique when she'd returned to the cottage after the accident, which had seemed utterly ridiculous. How could she have lived in a house for almost a decade and not remember where her bedroom was?

But it had all sunk in again eventually. And it

would happen here at Larkford too, if she had time and a little bit of peace and quiet so she could concentrate. She mentally thanked Charlie again for organising things so she could have a week here on her own before her boss arrived back from wherever that red carpet was. Had Charlie mentioned New York…?

As she wandered round, she was pleased to find that the inside of Larkford Place was as lovely as its exterior. It oozed character. No steel and glass ground-breaking interior design here, thank goodness. Just ornate fireplaces and plasterwork, high ceilings and ancient leaded windows.

Ellie's jaw clicked as she let out a giant yawn. Fatigue was a normal part of her condition—due to the fact she had to concentrate on things most people did automatically. And today had been a day that had required an awful lot of mental and emotional energy. No wonder she was ready to drop. It was time to check out the housekeeper's apartment above the old stables, so she could crash into bed and become blissfully unconscious.

She pulled a couple of bags out of the boot of her car as she passed it, and made her way up the stairs to her new home. But when she opened the door, the smell of damp carpet clogged her nostrils. And it wasn't hard to see why. Water was dripping through a sagging bulge in the ceiling, and the living room floor was on its way to becoming a decent-sized duck pond. There was no way she could sleep in here tonight.

So she dragged her bags back to the main house, up the stairs and into one of the guest rooms on the first floor. By the time she'd left a message with a local plumber and placed some kitchen pans underneath the damaged ceiling to catch the worst of the dripping water, the yawns were coming every five seconds. She only made it through half of her unpacking before she decided it was time to stop what she was doing and tootle down the hallway to the bathroom she'd spotted earlier before falling into bed.

But as she lay there in the dark, with only the creakings of the old house for company, she found she could close her eyelids but sleep was playing hide-and-seek. Running away from home had seemed such a good idea a few weeks ago, but now she was second-guessing her impulse.

What if she proved Charlie's unspoken fears to be right? What if she wasn't up to the job?

And she *needed* to be up to this job, she really did—for so many reasons.

She'd just about come to terms with the fact that the accident had not only destroyed her perfect family, it had also altered her brain permanently. She would never be the same person she'd been before that day, never be the Ellie she knew herself to be.

Sometimes it felt as if she were inhabiting the body of a stranger, and she could feel her old self staring over her shoulder, noticing the things she couldn't do any more, raising her eyebrows at the mood swings and the clumsiness.

She rolled over and tried another position. Was it possible to haunt yourself? She certainly hoped not. She had enough ghosts to outrun as it was.

She sighed and clutched the duvet a little closer to her chest.

Maybe she'd never be that person again, but this job was her lifeline, her chance to prove to herself and everyone else that she wasn't a waste of space. This was her chance to be *normal* again, away from the judging eyes and the sympathetic glances. She was just going to have to be the best darn house-keeper that Mr Mark Wilder had ever had.

As the awards ceremony dragged on Mark was proved right. It had been an *incredibly* long night.

Melodie was irritating him. The package was

pretty, but there wasn't much inside to interest him. He had tried to engage her in talk about the music industry, but even though she was trying to veer her career in that direction she seemed superbly uninformed about the business.

The show was good, but he had the feeling he'd seen it all before—the pseudo-feuds between cool, young indie bands, the grandpa rockers behaving badly as they presented awards and the hip-grinding dance routines by girls wearing little more than scarves. Well, maybe he didn't object to the skimpy dresses that much, he thought with a chuckle. He was tired, not *dead*.

The only highlight of the evening had been Kat's victory in the 'Best Newcomer' category. Nobody else might have noticed the way her hands shook as she held the supposedly funky-looking trophy, but Mark had. She'd accepted her award with simple thanks, then performed her latest single, sitting alone on the stage except for her guitar and a spotlight. The whole audience had been silent as her husky voice had permeated the sweaty atmosphere. When she'd finished, even the most jaded in the crowd of musicians and industry professionals had given her an ovation.

The remainder of the ceremony was a blur as

Mark tried to keep his eyes open. He began to regret the two glasses of champagne he'd drunk. He hadn't eaten since the flight this morning, and the alcohol was having a less than pleasant effect on him. Instead of mellowing him out, everything jarred. All he wanted to do was get home and sleep for a week solid.

The ceremony drew to a close and Kat leaned over to Mark. 'Are you coming to the after-show party?'

Melodie, who was eavesdropping, looked hopeful.

Mark shook his head. 'I'm tired and jet-lagged. I'm going home to bed.'

Melodie looked even more hopeful.

Erm...I don't think so, sweetheart.

It was time to ease himself out of the situation. Melodie would probably be happier at the party, mixing with the boy bands, anyway. He gave her a non-commital, nice-to-have-met-you kiss on the cheek. 'I know I'm being boring, but why don't you join the others at the party? I'm sure Kat and...er...'

'Razor,' said Kat helpfully.

'*Razor* will look after you.'

Melodie weighed her options up for a second, and decided the offer wasn't too shabby after all. 'That's cool,' she said in her little-girl voice and flicked her hair extensions.

Mark slipped away, leaving the theatre by the back exit, happy to distance himself from the muffled roar of the paparazzi as the stars emerged onto the red carpet out front. He fished his mobile phone out of his jacket pocket and called a cab, telling the driver to meet him in a backstreet close by, then ran a hand through his unruly mop of dark hair and made his way down an alley. Only when he had emerged from the shadow of the theatre did he loosen the top button of his shirt and breathe in a luxurious lungful of cool night air.

CHAPTER THREE

SO MUCH for sleeping for a week solid. Someone was making a racket on the landing. How inconsiderate could you get?

Mark sat up in bed, cold reality only just intruding on his nice, warm sleep haze.

After the awards ceremony he'd had the urge to get right out of the city, so instead of asking the cab driver to make the short trip to his flat on the river, Mark had made him very happy and told him the destination was Sussex.

There was another noise from the landing. Nothing loud, but someone was definitely out there. He hadn't dreamt it. There was only one explanation. It was after two in the morning and someone was in his house. Someone he hadn't invited because he was supposed to be here on his own. That wasn't good.

Mark jumped out of bed, wondering what he might have to hand in his bedroom that would help in a situation like this, but it was pitch-dark and he didn't have a clue where to start fumbling. He knew his squash racket was in the house somewhere…

But he didn't have time even to reach for the lamp by his bed. Just then the door slammed open. Mark tensed, unable to see who or what had just invaded his bedroom. A split-second later something—someone—barrelled into him.

He didn't have time to think, just reached out and grabbed him. There was no way some snotty youth from the village was going to swipe his silver, or his high-tech audio gear, or whatever it was he was after.

A struggle ensued and he finally got the lad pinned down on the floor. Now what? How was he going to call the police without—?

'Ow!'

A searing pain radiated from his right collar-bone. The little runt had bitten him! Actually sunk his teeth in and clenched hard! And now he was getting away, even though Mark didn't remember letting him go. He grabbed for the intruder and was rewarded with an ankle.

Well, it was better then nothing.

Time to take the upper hand. And the first thing was to see who he was dealing with. They were both shouting at each other—although it seemed to be more sounds than words that he was deciphering. He lunged for the bedside lamp and switched it on.

And that was when things really got confusing. Maybe he was dreaming after all.

This was no lad from the village. Not with those soft blonde ringlets and wide green eyes. And she was wearing…pyjamas! He flushed hot at the thought, though he hardly knew why. They were thick brushed cotton and only hinted at the curves beneath. Now, he knew some women could be a little over-keen to meet him, but this was just ridiculous!

And then she started babbling, and in the string of words he heard his own name.

'I know who I am. Who on earth are *you*?'

She looked up at him, breathless and blushing. The only motion he was aware of was the uneven rise and fall of the curves under her pyjama top; the only noise was their mingled rapid breathing. And then she spoke.

'I'm Ellie Bond—your new housekeeper.'

He'd been clenching his jaw in anger, but now it relaxed. His eyes widened as the sleep fog cleared from his brain. She pulled her arms and legs into herself and sat ball-like at his feet, suddenly looking like a little girl. She began to shiver.

Truth was, he had no idea how to handle this. And it was better if she got out of here before he said or did something he'd regret in the morning.

'You'd better get back to your room,' he said.

She should have known something was up when she'd tripped over that stray shoe. She never left her shoes lying around. And last night had been no different. She'd kicked them off and placed them neatly beside her case before going to bed. At home, her make-up might be spilled all over the dressing table, her jeans might be hanging by one leg over the back of a chair, but she always put her shoes away. Mainly because she only wore something on her feet when absolutely necessary. Her feet liked freedom.

Ellie stretched. Apparently a bulldozer had run over her last night while she'd drifted in and out of sleep—and then had reversed and had another go. There was no point trying to drop off again now. She was an early bird by nature and she knew her body clock would refuse.

She gave up squeezing her eyelids closed and rolled over and looked at the curtains. Dawn wasn't far away. Maybe some fresh air would stop her brain spinning in five different directions at once. She pulled a huge cable-knit sweater on over her pyjamas. Since she didn't own a pair of slippers she tugged a pair of flip-flops from the jumble at one end of her case.

Once she was ready she paused, listening for any hint of movement from the room next door. There was nothing.

Now she was satisfied the coast was clear, she headed into the hallway and stopped briefly to reassess the scene of the crime, counting the doors on this side of the corridor. Four. There was a small cupboard opposite the bathroom that she could have sworn hadn't been there before.

Not wanting to get caught in her pyjamas a second time, she turned in the opposite direction and went down the narrow staircase towards the kitchen, a room far enough away from the bedrooms for her to finally breathe out and think. Once there, she switched the kettle on and looked aimlessly round the room. The passageway that led into the cobbled courtyard was visible through the half-open door. Her car was sitting out there, ready to go. One of her mad impulses hit her.

What if she just ran out through the door this

minute, jumped in her car and bombed out of the front gates, never to be seen again? Tingles broke out all over her arms. The urge to do just that was positively irresistible. It was only six o' clock.

Breathe. Think...

She recognised this itchy feeling for what it was—another legacy of her head injury. It was all very well to know that her impulse control was permanently out of whack, but another thing entirely to tap into that knowledge when you were in the magnetic grip of what seemed like the best idea ever and find the strength to resist it.

She should be thankful, though. At least she was just a bit harum-scarum these days. Some of the other people she'd met during her rehabilitation had it far worse. How could she forget Barry, who didn't seem to realise that grabbing the rear end of every woman he clapped eyes on wasn't appropriate behaviour? Or Fenella, the posh old lady who swore like a trooper if she didn't have an even number of peas on her plate at dinnertime, all lined up in rows? Ellie nodded to herself. Oh, yes. Things could be a lot worse. She just had to keep remembering that.

As if she could forget, when last night's disastrous run-in with the boss was clearly going to get her fired.

She brewed herself a strong cup of tea and opened the French windows that led onto a wide patio. The garden was beautiful in the soft early-morning sunshine. She breathed deeply and walked along the smooth grey flagstones till she emerged from the shadow of the house into the warmth of the sunrise. She skirted the lavender hedge, sipping her mug of tea, and stepped onto a rectangle of lush, close-clipped grass. It was heavy with dew and springy underfoot. Her head fell back and she stayed motionless for a minute or so, feeling the sun's rays on her cheeks and inhaling the clean, pure scents of the awakening garden.

This reminded her of mornings at her cottage years ago. Sometimes she would wake early and sneak out into the garden before Sam and Chloe stirred. The garden had been Ellie's place to centre herself, to pause from the hectic pace of life and just *be*. She would walk out barefoot and let the soft blades of the lawn tickle her toes. Then she would wander about, clearing her head by talking out loud. Sometimes she just rambled to herself; sometimes she couldn't help looking skyward and thanking God for all the amazing things that made her life perfect.

When she returned to the cottage she would be

able to hear the machinery of the day starting to whirr—the clattering of toothbrushes in the bathroom, footsteps on the stairs. However busy the day got after that, she carried a sense of peace with her that had been born in the quiet of the day. It had been her secret ritual.

But she hadn't done it for years—not since Sam and Chloe had died. There was no peace to be found anywhere. Did she think she'd find it under a bush in her own back garden? Not likely. And as for God, she'd been tempted to stand outside late at night and scream at Him for being so cruel. They hadn't been on speaking terms since.

Ellie bent down to examine a cobweb glistening between the branches of a small shrub. Beads of moisture clinging to each strand reflected the sunlight like a thousand tiny mirrors.

What was she going to do? She was all alone and in a terrible mess. Her pretty dreams about being independent, free from the past, had come crashing down around her ears in less than twenty-four hours. What a fool she'd been to think she could outrun her ghosts.

A tear bulged in the corner of her eye. She sniffed and wiped it away with her middle finger. Thoughts were scrambling around inside her head, so she stood still and let the spring sun warm her inside and out. Then, when she was ready, she shook off her flip-flops and walked, and talked to the faultless blue sky until the words ran dry.

A floorboard on the landing creaked. Ellie stopped stuffing clothes randomly into bags and held her breath at the back of her throat.

She'd heard noises upstairs some time after noon, and had scurried up here not long after that. It was amazing just how long it could take a person to pack two cases and a couple of smaller bags. She'd made it last all afternoon.

But for once her reasoning panned out: the longer she left it before she saw him again, the less embarrassed she would feel and the easier it would be to handle her emotions when he asked her to leave. It couldn't hurt to delay the inevitable confrontation with her soon-to-be-ex-boss until she'd finished packing and was on an even keel.

She squashed the T-shirt she was holding into the case in front of her and reached for her wash bag. It slid out of her fingers, but she managed to snatch at it, gripping it between forefinger and thumb before it reached the floor. Unfortunately her quick reflexes didn't stop the contents spilling out and scattering all over the rug. With all her limbs occupied just preventing the bag from falling, she couldn't do anything but watch as her tube of toothpaste bounced on the floor, then disappeared deep under the bed.

So much for an even keel. The world was still stubbornly off-kilter and refusing to go right side up.

She lifted Chloe's blue teddy from where she'd placed it on her pillow the night before and pressed it to her face. For a while it had smelled of her daughter, but the scent of strawberry shampoo had long since faded. Ellie kissed it with reverence and placed it beside the case.

She'd only allowed herself a few treasures from home, and they had been the first things she'd pulled from her luggage when she'd unpacked. Propped on the bedside table was a single silver picture frame. The photo it held was her favourite of her and Sam together, taken on their honeymoon. They'd handed their camera to the retired couple in the next hotel room and asked them to take a snap on the day they'd travelled home.

She preferred this picture to the forced poses of her wedding photos. They were laughing at each other, hair swept sideways by the wind, not even aware of the exact moment the shutter had opened. She traced a finger over her husband's cheek.

Her beautiful Sam.

He had been so warm and funny, with his lopsided grin and wayward hair. When he'd died it had been like losing a vital organ. Living and breathing were just so hard without him.

They'd met on the first day of primary school and been inseparable ever since, marrying one week after they'd both graduated from university. Sam had taken a teaching post at the village school and she'd commuted to the City, working as a PA for a big City firm, and they'd saved to buy the rundown cottage on the outskirts that they'd fallen in love with. They'd transformed the tumble-down wreck bit by bit, scouring architectural salvage yards for stained glass, old taps and doorknobs. They had even rescued an old roll-top bath out of one of their neighbour's gardens—removing the geraniums before it was plumbed in.

When the last lick of paint had dried, they had proclaimed it their dream home and immediately started trying for a family. The following spring, they'd come home from the hospital with Chloe, a tiny pink bundle with fingers and toes so cute they'd verged on the miraculous. Ellie had almost felt guilty about being more happy than a person had a right to be.

But one wet afternoon had robbed her of all of it.

Her smile dissolved and she pushed the frame flat and folded the photo up in her pyjamas before tucking it into a well-padded corner of her sturdiest case.

When she'd moved back home after her rehabilitation, well-meaning friends and family had taken one of two approaches—some had wanted her to freeze-frame time and never do anything, the rest had dropped great clanging hints at her feet about moving on with her life. Their insensitivity had astounded her.

Move on? She hadn't wanted to move on! She'd wanted things back the way they were *before*. Chloe's pink wellies in the hallway. Sam bent over the kitchen table marking homework. But that was impossible. So she'd settled for hibernating in the present. But hibernating hadn't taken long to become festering. Perhaps she should be glad that events in the village had forced her to leave.

She zipped up her bulging case, then sat on the edge of the bed and stared at the elegant surroundings.

Her journey had led her here, to Larkford Place. Unfortunately only a brief pit-stop. She hadn't a clue what she'd do next. She could stay at the cottage for a few weeks if there weren't any holiday bookings. But that would be going back, and now she was finally ready to move forward she didn't want to do that.

However, she didn't really have much choice after last night.

It was time she hauled her things down to the car. She picked up a case in one hand and stuffed a smaller one under her other arm, leaving her hand free to open the door. She tugged it open and froze.

Mark Wilder was standing straight in front of her, fist bunched ready as if to knock.

Mark dropped his hand, stuffed it in his back pocket and pulled out a wad of folded twenty-pound notes. He held them out to Ellie.

'I thought you might need this.'

She stared at him as if he was offering her a hand grenade.

'For the shopping,' he added.

'Shopping?'

'Yes. Shopping. You know, with money…'

He waved the notes in front of her chin. Her

eyes moved left and right, left and right, following the motion of his hand.

'Money?'

This was harder work than he'd thought it would be.

'Yes. Money. It's what we use in the civilised world when we've run out of camels to barter with.'

'But I thought…' She fidgeted with a small silver locket hanging round her neck. 'You'd…I'd be…'

Colour flared on her cheeks and she stepped away from him. He looked at the notes in his hand. She didn't seem to understand the concept of shopping, which was a definite minus in a house-keeper. His decision to view last night as an embarrassing one-off started to seem premature.

He stepped through the door frame and followed her into the room. There were cases and bags on the bed. They were lumpy enough to look as if they had been filled in a hurry. The zips weren't done up all the way, and something silky was falling out of the holdall nearest to him. He really should stop looking at it.

Ellie followed his gaze and dived for the bag, stuffing the item back in so deep that most of her arm disappeared. Now he was just staring at a pile of cases.

Cases? He tilted his head. Oh. Right. She thought he was going to give her the sack.

Well, as tempting as the idea might be, he couldn't afford to do that at present. Firstly because he'd never hear the end of it from Charlie, and secondly because he really did need someone here to look after the house while he was travelling. He was due on another plane in less than twenty-four hours and he simply didn't have the luxury of finding someone else. It had been hard enough to fill the position at short notice when Mrs Timms had decided to leave.

Maybe it was time to work some of the legendary Wilder magic and put this Ellie Bond at ease. If he showed her he was laughing off the incident last night, it might help her relax.

Mark waited for her to finish fiddling with the bag, and then pulled a smile out of his arsenal—the one guaranteed to melt ice maidens at fifty paces.

'Well, I'm glad to see you're still in your own room, anyway.' He threw in a wink, just to make sure she knew he was joking. 'With your track record, we can't be too careful.'

Hmm. Strange. Nothing happened. No thaw whatsoever.

'There's no need to go on about that. It's just that

I wasn't expecting anyone else to be here, and I'm not familiar with the layout of the house yet, and I just…the moon went in…I counted three instead of four…' The babbling continued.

There was one thing that was puzzling him. If she'd wanted a bathroom, why had she trekked down the hall?

'Why didn't you just use the *en-suite*?'

She stopped mid-babble. *'En-suite?'*

He walked over to a cream-coloured panelled door on the opposite wall to the bed, designed to match the wardrobe on the other side of the chimney breast. He nudged it gently with his knuckles and it clicked open. Her jaw lost all muscle tone as she walked slowly towards the compact but elegant bathroom.

She shook her head, walked in, looked around and walked out again, still blessedly silent. Actually, his new housekeeper seemed relatively normal when she stopped biting and yelling and babbling.

He had a sudden flashback to the night before—to the baggy blue and white pyjamas that hadn't been quite baggy enough to disguise her curves—and he started to get a little flustered himself.

'I have a…bathroom…inside my wardrobe?'

He gave a one-shouldered shrug. 'Actually, it's not quite as Narnia-like as it seems. The wardrobe is that side.' He pointed to an identical cream door the other side of the chimney breast. 'We just had the door to the *en-suite* built to match. Secret doors seem to suit a house like this.'

The look on her face told him she thought it was the stupidest idea ever.

'I thought it was fun,' he said, willing her to smile back at him, to join him in a little light banter and laugh the whole thing off as an unfortunate first meeting. She just blinked.

'Anyway,' he continued with a sigh, 'let's just see if we can get through the next twenty-four hours without something—or someone—going bump in the night.'

'I told you before. It was an accident,' she said, scrunching her forehead into parallel lines.

It looked as if she was tempted to bite him again. Humour was obviously not the way to go. Back to business, then. That had to be safe territory, didn't it?

'Okay, well take this for now.' He placed the money on the chest of drawers while she watched him suspiciously. 'I'm getting a credit card sorted out for the household expenses, and a laptop so we can keep in touch via e-mail. I just need you to sign a few forms, if that's all right?'

She nodded, but her eyes never left him, as if she was expecting him to make a sudden move.

Mark wandered over to the bed, picked up the sad-looking blue bear sitting next to one of the cases and gave it a cursory inspection. He wouldn't have expected her to be the sort who slept with a teddy, but, hey, whatever rocked her boat. He tossed it back on the bed. It bounced and landed on the floor. Ellie rushed to scoop it up, clutched it to her chest and glared at him.

He raked his fingers through his hair. It was time to beat a hasty retreat.

'I'll see you at dinner, then?' He raised his hands on a non-threatening gesture. An insane image of him as a lion tamer, holding off a lioness with a rickety old chair, popped into his head. He wouldn't be surprised if she growled at him.

'Fine.' It almost *was* a growl.

'Would you join us? I've invited Charlie to dinner, to say thank you for finding me a—'

The word *hellcat* had been poised to fall out of his mouth and he stopped himself just in time.

Not hellcat. Housekeeper! Just try and remember that.

'—for finding me a *housekeeper* at such short notice. I thought it would be a good way to break the ice before I disappear again.'

'Thank you,' she said. Her eyes told him she'd rather walk on hot coals.

Fine. If she wanted to keep it cool and impersonal, he could keep it cool and impersonal. Probably.

'If you could be ready to serve up at eight o'clock…?'

Her eyes narrowed almost imperceptibly.

He backed out through the door and started walking towards the main staircase. Charlie had a lot to answer for. Her perfect-for-the-job friend was perfectly strange, for one thing! He took himself downstairs and sat on the velvet-covered sofa in front of the fire. Jet lag was making it hard to think, and he had the oddest feeling that his conversation with Ellie had just been weird enough for him still to be asleep and dreaming.

She was clearly barking mad. If the 'lost-my-bedroom' incident had planted a seed of suspicion in his mind, their talk just now and what he had seen early this morning had definitely added fertiliser.

His body clock was still refusing to conform to Greenwich Mean Time, and last night he'd dozed, tossed and turned, read some of a long-winded novel and eventually decided on a hot shower to clear his head. On the way to his bathroom a flash of movement outside the window had prompted him to change course and peer out of the half-open curtains.

Down in the garden he'd spotted Ellie, marching round the garden, arms waving. She'd been talking to herself! At six in the morning. In her pyjamas.

Pyjamas.

Another rush of something warm and not totally unfamiliar hit him. The pleasant prickle of aware-ness from the close proximity of a woman was one of the joys of life. But he didn't think he'd ever experienced it after seeing a woman wearing what looked to be her grandad's pyjamas before. Silk and satin, yes. Soft stripy brushed cotton, no. There it went again! The rush. His earlobes were burning, for goodness' sake!

He'd practically had a heart attack when she'd charged into him in the dark last night. He'd been in such a deep sleep only moments before he'd hardly known *who* he was, let alone *where* he was. The small frame and slender wrists of his captive might have fooled him into thinking it was a lad he'd held captive, but when the light had flickered on he'd realised he couldn't have been more wrong. It certainly hadn't been a boy he had by the ankle, intent on dragging him down to the local police station. He'd started to wonder if he'd been dreaming. Those soft blonde curls belonged on a Botticelli cherub.

Just then the bite mark on his left shoulder began to throb.

No, not an angel—his instincts had been right from the start. A hellcat.

It would be wise to remind himself of that. He didn't have to like this woman; he just had to pay her to keep his house running. He would keep his distance from Ellie Bond and he would not think of her in that way—even if there was something refreshingly different about her.

Insanity, he reminded himself. *That's what's different about her. A woman like that is trouble. You never know what she's going to do next.*

A yawn crept up on him. He told himself it would be a bad idea to fall asleep again, but there was something very soothing about watching the logs in the fire crackle and spark. He pushed a cushion under his head and settled to watch the flames shimmer and dance.

When he opened his eyes again the flames had disappeared and the embers were just grey dust. Now and then a patch of orange would glow brightly, then fade away again. He pulled himself out of the comfortable dent he had created in the sofa.

From somewhere in the direction of the kitchen he could hear female voices. Was Charlie here already? He looked at his watch. He'd been asleep for more than three hours. He walked towards the dining room and met Charlie, coming to fetch him. His stomach gurgled. His sleep patterns might be sabotaged, but his appetite was clearly on Larkford time.

'Now, don't go upsetting my friend, Mark. She needs this job, and you are not allowed to mess it up for her.'

Hang on a second. He was the employer. Surely this was all supposed to be the other way round? Ellie was supposed to do a good job for *him*, try not to upset *him*. At the moment he was wondering whether his house would still be standing when he returned in a few weeks.

He opened his mouth to say as much, then decided not to bother. There was no arguing with his bossy cousin when she got like this. It had been the same when he'd tried to talk her out of taking a stray kitten home one summer, when he'd been fourteen and she'd been ten. Charlie had worshipped that cat, but he'd never quite forgotten the lattice of fine red marks the animal had left on his hands and forearms after he'd agreed to carry it back to the house for her.

Unfortunately it had taken another twenty years before he'd been cured of the habit of trying to rescue pathetic strays of all shapes and sizes.

Helena had been like that. Soft, fragile-looking, vulnerable. And he hadn't been able to resist her. Something inside him swelled with protective instinct when he came across women like that. And Helena had been the neediest of them all. Not that he'd minded. He would have gladly spent all his days looking after her.

Three months after Charlie had found the kitten, when its tummy was round and its fur had a healthy sheen, it had disappeared and never come back. That was the problem with strays. It was in their nature to be selfish.

So he avoided strays altogether now, both feline *and* female.

Oh, women always wanted *something* from him. But he made them play by his rules, only mixing with women who wanted simpler things: money, fame by association, attention. Those things were easy to give and cost him nothing.

Mark was pulled back to the present by the aroma of exotic herbs and spices wafting his way. Charlie didn't need to steer him any more. The smell was a homing beacon, leading him up the corridor and into the dining room. He dropped into a chair opposite Charlie and waited, all his taste buds on full alert.

There was a glimpse of an apron and blonde hair through the doorway as Ellie disappeared back into the kitchen to fetch the last in a succession of steaming dishes. Mark swallowed the pool of saliva that had collected in the bottom of his mouth. He hoped she wouldn't be too long.

She finally appeared. At least he thought it was her. She was cool and collected and quiet, and set down the last dish in an array of lavish Thai recipes. Not a hint of growling or biting about her.

Good. He was glad she'd pulled herself together.

His stomach, however, didn't care how the transformation had happened. It grumbled at him to just get over it and start shovelling food in its general direction. Which he did without delay.

CHAPTER FOUR

ELLIE dished up. Her heart jumped so hard in her chest she was sure the serving spoon must be pulsing in her fingers. What was happening to her? Mark Wilder had done nothing but walk into the room and sit down and her body had gone wild. She finished doling out the food and sat down, careful to keep her eyes on her plate lest her stampeding hormones concentrate themselves and get ready for another charge.

The man was *insanely* good-looking!

The TV cameras hadn't done him justice at all. No longer did she want to scold the reporter for drooling; she wanted to congratulate her for forming a coherent sentence.

Last night she'd been too shocked to register the weird physiological response he provoked in her, and this afternoon she'd been too angry. At herself, mainly, but she'd vented at him instead. It was her stupid brain injury that was to blame.

She'd never had problems with runaway emotions before that. Now, any little thing could trigger overwhelming frustration, or rage, or despair.

Of course! She'd inadvertently stumbled upon the answer.

Her sigh of relief drew glances from her dining companions. She caught Mark's eye and quickly returned her gaze to the king prawn on the end of her fork while she waited for her heartbeat to settle.

How could she not have remembered?

The doctors had warned her that some people noticed a change to their sex drive after a traumatic head injury. This intense attraction, this wobbly feeling, it was all down to her head injury. She didn't like him *that way* at all, really. It was just her stupid neurons getting themselves in knots because of the damage they'd suffered.

What a relief!

It explained everything. She could never normally be attracted to a man like him—a man so…well, she didn't have words for what he was *so*… But she'd never seen the attraction of bad boys. Who needed the heartache? Give her a man like Sam—warm, dependable, *faithful*—any day. Not a charmer who thought everything with two X chromosomes ought to fall at his feet and worship.

Now she had that sorted out in her head she could relax a little and enjoy the food. But as she ate questions started to float to the surface.

Why now?

Why, after four years of seeming perfectly normal in that department—even completely uninterested at times—had this symptom decided to rear its ugly head?

It didn't matter. Whatever the reason, she needed to get a handle on it. This job was important to her and she didn't want to lose it. She'd just have to read up a bit on the subject, introduce measures to cope with it, just like she had with her other symptoms. By the time he got back from his next trip she'd have it completely under control.

She made the mistake of glancing up at that point, just as Mark smiled at something Charlie said. He wasn't even looking at her, for goodness' sake, but Ellie still felt her body straining at the leash.

Down, girl!

Oh, my. This evening was going to be torture.

Thankfully, she had an excuse to keep herself busy. She would pay attention to the food, and only the food. And when the meal was over she'd plead tiredness and escape to her room. Charlie would understand. She'd have to.

* * *

Mark stole a handful of looks at Ellie as the clattering of serving spoons gave way to silence. She kept her eyes on her plate, only lifting them once to dish out another spoonful of rice.

The only information she'd volunteered during dinner had been about the plumbing disaster in the housekeeper's apartment, which cleared up the final mystery of why she'd been sleeping in the room next door to his. She'd barely acknowledged his thanks for organizing the repairs.

So much for 'breaking the ice'. It seemed the dining room was in the grip of a rapidly advancing cold snap. But he wasn't going to push.

Instead, he turned to Charlie and asked after her brother, which led to a raft of hilarious anecdotes about his recent backpacking trip to Indonesia.

Ellie said nothing. It was almost as if she knew she was sitting a few feet away from him but was desperately trying to wish herself invisible, or at the very least make herself blend into the background. Whatever she was trying to do, it wasn't working.

It was odd. She wore virtually no make-up, and the reckless curls were piled on top of her head and secured with a clip, and yet he couldn't stop glancing at her. It must be pheromones or something, because she wasn't his usual type at all.

Not any more, anyway.

A curl escaped from the long silver clip on top of Ellie's head and threatened to dunk itself in her meal, but before it could slim fingers tucked it behind her ear. That tiny hand had packed quite a punch last night. He stared at it, watched her fingers as they pleated her serviette, closed around her fork…

Charlie caught him with his cutlery frozen between his mouth and his plate, eyes fixed on Ellie. She smirked. He retaliated with a warning kick under the table. He knew how much of a blabbermouth Charlie was, and he didn't want her complicating things by teasing him, especially as he and Ellie had reached an icy truce. Besides, there was nothing to tease him about. She was his housekeeper.

Charlie glared at him and leaned underneath the table to rub her leg. A second later searing pain radiated from his shinbone.

'Ouch!'

Ellie glanced up, puzzled by the exchange, and Mark decided to deflect the attention from himself before she realised the food wasn't the only thing that was causing his mouth to fill with saliva.

He could do polite and businesslike. He could behave like a proper employer rather than a best buddy. And, with a sideways look at his cousin, he decided to prove it.

'So… Where are you from, Ellie?'

Ellie chased some glass noodles round her plate. Mark stretched out, then rested his hands behind his head and waited.

'Kent,' she replied quietly.

'The whole of Kent, or one spot in particular?'

'Barkleigh.'

What was that edge in her voice? Was she angry with him?

That was a little unfair. After all, she wasn't the one with teeth marks on her torso. And he'd done his best to wave the olive branch by chatting to her earlier on, and got his head bitten off for his trouble.

Pity. He liked a woman with a sense of humour.

Cancel that thought. She was an employee. He was her boss. He would make polite conversation and help her to feel more comfortable, right? Good. *Here goes…*

'So, what made you decide to—?'

Ellie clattered the empty plates together before he could finish his sentence and vanished in the direction of the kitchen, muttering something about coffee. Mark waited a split second, then grabbed a couple of empty wine glasses as an excuse to follow her. He got the distinct impression he'd said something wrong, although he couldn't think what it might be. His questions had been innocent enough—bland, even.

When he got to the kitchen Ellie was standing motionless near the sink, a couple of dishes still in her hands. She looked lost. Not in a metaphorical sense, but genuinely lost—as if she'd suddenly found herself in alien territory and had no idea of what to do or where to go next. Mark stepped forward to help her, and she jumped as if electricity had arced between them. The crockery leapt out of her arms and smashed against the flagstone floor.

She stammered her apologies and started to pick up the pieces.

'No. It was my fault,' he said. 'I startled you.'

He bent down to help her. She looked across at him as they both crouched beside the kitchen cabinets, picking up the remnants of the dishes. Their knees almost grazed, and whatever had startled her shot through him too. An anonymous emotion flickered in her eyes and she looked away.

When they had finished clearing away the mess, he pulled out one of the kitchen stools and motioned for her to sit down.

'I'll do the coffee.'

Her eyes opened wide, and he could feel the heat of her stare as he turned to the coffee machine.

'Dinner was stupendous,' he said as he placed a cup and saucer in front of her.

'Thank you,' she replied, looking even more surprised.

Suddenly he didn't feel like being the normal, wise-cracking Mark Wilder everyone expected him to be. He didn't want to *dazzle*. Some forgotten instinct told him to pare it all back, leave the charm behind and just talk to her, human being to human being. Actually, he did have something he wanted to ask her, something that might cement them in their right relationship without causing her to take offence.

'Actually, I was wondering if you could do me a favour.'

Her eyebrows raised a notch further.

'I mean, I love exotic food, but there is one thing I haven't had for a long time and I've *really* got a hankering for. I wonder if you wouldn't mind putting it on the menu some time?'

She looked at him, her eyes hooded and wary. 'What's that?'

He looked at floor before giving her a hopeful smile. 'Shepherd's Pie?'

Ellie Bond surprised him once again. Instead of scowling or rolling her eyes, she let go of all the tension she'd been holding in her face and laughed.

The kitchen was silent and empty when Ellie entered it the following morning. Dawn had come and gone, but the overcast sky produced an artificial twilight in the unlit kitchen. The state-of-the-art stainless steel appliances and barren worktop made the place look like a hotel. There was none of the usual clutter that made a kitchen the heart of the home. No family photos. No children's drawings. No pet bowls.

She found a note on the counter from Mark, letting her know he'd already left for the airport. An itinerary was stapled to it, in case she needed to contact him while he was away. She read the note in full, and cheered up instantly when she discovered he'd given her permission to buy anything she needed for the kitchen. Some women loved shopping for shoes; Ellie had a worrying love of shopping for kitchen gadgets—and this house could definitely do with her attention. It needed a food processor and measuring spoons and a griddle… And that was just for starters. It wasn't that there wasn't anything in the cupboards, but most of the equipment fell into the 'pretty but useless' category. The designer grater she'd found had been an odd shape, and they'd almost feasted on grated knuckles instead of grated ginger in their curry last night.

Outside it was grey and chilly, but the grounds of Larkford were still beautiful. Daffodils—not the garish ones, but blooms the colour of clotted cream—had burst through the lawn in clumps and were now whispering cheerfully to each other in the breeze. Wood pigeons cooed in the trees, and the first cherry blossoms were now visible on the silvery grey branches. It was almost a shame to be inside, so she went out for a walk, and continued walking long after the bottom of her teacup was visible.

Taking her cup of tea for a walk became part of her morning routine. On her return to the kitchen she would pass the super-duper, multi-highlighted calendar on the large fridge and mentally tick off the days until Mark returned.

Twelve more days of blissful solitude… Eleven more days… Eight more days…

And she ignored the fact that she felt slightly elated, rather than disappointed, as each day went by.

Mark lounged on a wicker sofa, high on the roof terrace of his hotel's penthouse suite. He was ignoring the traffic rushing round the corner and down Rodeo Drive in favour of the clear blue sky above his head. It had been an extremely long day schmoozing record company executives and their sharp-toothed lawyers in order to finalise the launch of Kat's album in the US, but he'd come away with what he'd wanted from the meeting—eventually. He was very good at schmoozing, after all.

He'd had an invitation to go clubbing this evening, with a rather strait-laced lawyer who looked as if she'd be a whole lot of fun once she let loose, but he'd turned her down. For some reason he wanted to be on his own at the moment. He didn't feel right, and he needed to relax a little and work out why.

Today he felt out of sorts, uncomfortable. As if he was wearing a suit that wasn't cut quite right. He closed his eyes and sank into the deep cushions of the sofa.

Well, he wasn't wearing a suit now. He'd changed into shorts and a T-shirt as soon as he'd got back to his suite. Unfortunately he still had that same itchy feeling, as if something wasn't quite right. He shook his head and pulled his sunglasses down over his eyes. Even with them closed the sun was still a little bright, burning strange shapes onto the backs of his eyelids.

Slowly the blobs swam and merged, until they solidified into an image that looked suspiciously familiar. In fact it looked suspiciously like his new housekeeper. He snapped his lids open and let the white sun bleach his retina instead.

What was up with him?

This was the third time something similar had happened. He was seeing her everywhere. And he didn't want to remember how sad and lost she'd looked when she'd smashed his best crockery to smithereens. He also didn't want to remember how warm and alive she'd looked when he'd mentioned Shepherd's Pie and she'd thrown her head back and laughed.

Housekeepers weren't supposed to be memorable. They were supposed to fade into the background and just do their job. He knew from personal experience how important it was to keep the lines between personal and professional firmly in place.

Somewhere in the back of his head he heard laughing.

Like you're doing with Kat?

That was different. He wasn't going to make the same mistake with Kat that he'd made with Nuclear Hamster. Stupid name. He'd advised them against it, but they hadn't listened. It was just that Kat was so young, she needed—

Okay, he was starting to act like a big brother towards Kat, but it didn't mean anything. Most importantly, it didn't mean he was setting a precedent of getting too close to his employees. He'd been cured of that fault a long time ago. Which meant he was totally capable of interacting with Ellie Bond without thinking of her as a woman—a woman who filled a pair of striped pyjamas very nicely, actually.

He sighed. He'd be back at Larkford in just over a week.

And Ellie would be there. It was what he'd hired her for, after all.

Suddenly the thought of the two of them alone in that big old house together seemed a little…intimate. He stood up, walked over to the parapet and stared out towards the Hollywood hills. A house like his—well, what it really needed was to be filled with people. Lots of them.

On the day there were only five spaces left on the calendar Ellie got restless. All her tasks were done, and she'd finished the book she was reading. She needed something to do. Something to clean out. Sorting through cupboards and purging the rubbish was a therapeutic activity she rather enjoyed. It made her feel as if she were in control of something for once.

The infamous cupboard opposite the bathroom had become the object of her obsession. As far as she could see it was full of boxes of miscellaneous clutter that had been sent down from Mark's London flat and had yet to be sorted out. She'd found plenty of bedlinen, a squash racket and three boxes of books. The empty shelves in the study came to mind, so Ellie decided to liberate the volumes from the dust and cardboard and put them where they could be useful.

She carried the box down to the study and started pulling books out and putting them on the thick wooden shelves. As she got to the last book in one stack a slip of paper fell out of the pages and wafted to the floor. She picked it up and realised it wasn't a piece of paper after all, but a photograph.

Not any old photograph. It was a wedding picture.

Mark and an anonymous bride.

Well, well, who'd have thought it? The bachelor playboy hadn't always been a bachelor. Bet he'd always been a playboy, though.

She frowned almost instinctively and studied the photograph more carefully. Mark looked younger—maybe in his mid-twenties?—fresh-faced, and very much in love with his beautiful, sophisticated bride. Her expression softened a little. A man who could look at a woman like that *had* something. Exactly what, she didn't know. Maybe he didn't either, because he'd thrown it all away and was living a very different life now. What a pity.

Turning the picture over, she saw the words 'Mark and Helena' scrawled on the back. The date underneath was twelve years earlier. Ellie slid the photograph back into its resting place and put the book on the shelf, feeling a little bit guilty for having found out what she sensed was a secret.

She reached for the next book, but was interrupted by the shrill beckoning of the telephone—the house line, not the one here in Mark's office.

Blast! She'd noticed the cradle in the hall was empty when she'd walked past with the box of books. She'd probably left the phone lying around again, which meant it might be anywhere.

She stood still and listened carefully.

The kitchen.

She raced down the passageway, skidding on the tiles in her socks.

It's in here somewhere!

The ringing was louder now, but oddly muffled. She ransacked a corner of the kitchen near the hob. Nothing! She leant closer to the worktop, then started frantically opening drawers.

Nope. Nope. Aha!

There it was, nestled amongst the wooden spoons. Where else?

She jabbed the button and uttered a breathless hello, then snapped to attention as she heard Mark's deep tones.

At first she didn't listen to the words, the content of what he was saying, because she hadn't been prepared for the way even his voice made her tingle. Oh, why couldn't he have e-mailed her? She wouldn't have had to concentrate on sounding normal if she'd been typing a reply!

Ah, but the phone call might have something

to do with the fact she'd forgotten her password and hadn't been able to check her e-mails for a while.

It was just then that she realised Mark had stopped talking.

'Ellie?'

'Uh-huh?'

'Are you…? Is everything all right?' She could hear him suppressing a smile.

Unfortunately she was more than a little breath-less—from all the phone-hunting, of course.

'Just…couldn't…find the phone.' She took a gulp of air and managed to croak, 'Can I help you?'

'Yep. I've decided to throw an impromptu party as a kind of housewarming when I get home. Only a few dozen guests—don't worry.'

A few dozen?

'My PA is handling the invites, and I'll get her to send you a list of caterers. We've decided on Saturday.'

'Saturday? This Saturday? That's less than a week away!'

'I know. I've been e-mailing for days, but you didn't reply. Don't stress. That'll be plenty of— hang on—'

Ellie huffed and tapped the counter as Mark

chatted to someone on his end of the line. She thought she heard a woman's voice.

None of my business. I don't care who he's with.

'Got to go, Ellie. I'll be back on Friday evening.'

The receiver hummed in her ear.

He hadn't even given her time to tell him that she couldn't possibly organise a party in six days. She'd only just got to grips with the day-to-day running of the house, and the last thing she needed was something that was going to send all that into a tailspin.

However, it didn't seem as if she had much choice. If she wanted to keep this job she would have to cater to her boss's whims, no matter how inconvenient.

Catering.

Was that the best place to start? It was so long since she'd had a social life herself, thinking about planning a party seemed as run-of-the-mill as planning a trek up the Amazon.

She closed her eyes. Remember what you learned at the support group. Don't panic over the big picture. Take things one step at a time. Start with the obvious.

Her eyelids lifted again. The cleaners were coming on Friday anyway, so no problem there.

And she could get Jim the gardener to help her re-arrange the furniture in the downstairs reception rooms, and the florists in the village could provide some arrangements.

After her initial panic she realised it wasn't that different from what she'd done when she'd worked as a PA in the City after leaving college. Her cantankerous boss had had a penchant for drop-of-the-hat cocktail parties to impress the partners, where he would swan round being all sweetness and light, then return to being a sour-faced grump the next day. If she could create a party to blow Martin Frobisher's socks off, she could certainly succeed with a lovely backdrop like Larkfield.

Yes, but that was *before*…

Shut up, she told herself. It's all there inside your head still. She was just going to have to do a little…archaeology to uncover the buried bits.

She could do this.

Her brain began to whirr with excitement as menu ideas sprang up in her mind. This was her chance to prove to Mark Wilder that she wasn't a loose cannon, that she could do this job.

She reached for the phonebook and flipped it open to 'F' for florists, her smile wide. Passwords could wait for later. For now she would use the phone.

If Mr Wilder wanted a party, she was going to give him a party!

Ellie slipped the straps of the little black dress she'd borrowed from Charlie over her shoulders. She wasn't looking forward to this evening one bit. She'd tried hard to talk him out of it, but Mark had insisted she attend the party—partly to keep an eye on the caterers and whatnot, but partly to 'have a bit of fun'. She'd have much preferred to stay holed up in her apartment with a packet of biscuits and a chick-flick.

She smoothed the bodice of the dress over her torso and looked in the mirror. She turned from one side to the other, scrutinising her reflection. Not bad. The simply cut black dress accentuated her curves, but didn't cling in desperation. She slipped on a pair of strappy high heels—also borrowed from Charlie. Her ankles wobbled as she adjusted to the altitude.

Tyres crunched on the gravel outside. She exhaled wearily. Guests were starting to arrive, which meant it was her cue to go downstairs. While it wasn't her place to welcome the guests, she wanted to make sure that the pair of local girls she'd hired to help with coats and suchlike had retained the pertinent information from their briefing yesterday.

Perhaps she could just stick it out for an hour or so and then slope off when he—when *no one*—was looking.

She left her room and headed for the main staircase. It wound down into a hall that was larger than the living room in her cottage. The banisters were solid oak, and still as sturdy as the day they'd been made. Ellie was rather grateful for them as she made her way down the stairs in Charlie's disobedient shoes. They seemed to have a mind of their own. She watched each foot carefully as she planted it on the next step, and it was only as she neared the bottom that she looked up and caught a glimpse of Mark, standing by the huge marble fireplace, chatting to the first of the arrivals.

Unfortunately she'd discovered when he'd returned home the previous evening that time and distance had done nothing to dilute the sheer physical impact the man had on her. It was pathetic, really, it was. She knew better, knew what sort of man he was, and yet here she was, *twittering* along with every other female in a five-

mile radius. She comforted herself with the knowledge that at least she had a medical reason for
behaving this way.

She looked over at Tania and Faith, the girls
from the village. Neither of them had thought to
relieve any guest of a coat or a wrap; they were too
busy standing in the corner and getting all giggly
over a certain member of the male species.

Ellie forced herself not to look at Mark as she
made her way across the hall and reissued her instructions to the two girls in a low, authoritative
voice. They instantly sprang into action, relieving
guests of their outerwear and delivering the items
to one of the smaller rooms on the ground floor
where Ellie had set up some portable clothing racks.

The only problem was that Tania and Faith were
now so intent on proving themselves efficient they'd
both darted off at once, leaving Ellie no choice but
to act as hat-check girl herself when the next huddle
of guests piled through the door. She approached the
group that had just crossed the threshold.

Mark moved forward to greet them at the same
time, and Ellie couldn't avoid meeting his gaze. It
was like being hit in the chest with one of those
Taser guns. Her heart stuttered, fizzing with a
million volts, and she disguised the resultant

quivering in her limbs by breaking eye contact and smoothing out a non-existent wrinkle on her dress. All the same, the hairs at the back of her neck lifted, full of static. She just knew he was still looking at her. He inhaled, as if he was about to say something, but before the words left his mouth, another voice gatecrashed the moment.

'Mark, you old dog!' bellowed a good-looking blond man in a dinner jacket, slapping him across the shoulders.

'Hello, Piers,' Mark replied in his good-humoured tone. 'Come in and find yourself a drink. What do you think of my new place?'

'Bloody difficult to find, that's what I say!' he roared, slapping Mark a second time.

Ellie was standing there still waiting to take any coats. She felt like a prize lemon.

'Let me introduce you to this trinity of lovelies,' Piers continued, ushering a group of bejewelled women into the house. 'Carla, Jade, and of course you already know Melodie.'

Of course. Ellie recognised her as the woman from the television. She didn't say anything, but silently willed Melodie to hurry up and hand that pashmina over. Ellie wanted an excuse to make herself scarce.

Mark didn't falter as he offered a polite greeting to all three women, but Ellie had a sense as she took hold of their wraps and coats that he wasn't as comfortable as his relaxed stance implied. She was just about to scamper away to the temporary cloakroom when the pair of girls returned and relieved her of her only legitimate means of escape.

Then, just to make matters worse, Mark turned to her and asked her something. She saw his lips move, heard the words, but her brain retained none of the information. Why had he done that? She was the help. And she'd actually like to keep their relationship on that footing, thank you very much. Things were complicated enough as it was.

Just then a waitress with a large tray walked past the entrance hall en-route to the drawing room. Caterers! She was supposed to be here in a professional capacity, after all. She would inspect each and every trayful of over-priced morsels and make sure they were just what she'd ordered. She mumbled something about food, not so much to Mark but to the room in general, then fell into step behind the waitress, lengthening the distance between her and the group at the doorway. As she rounded the corner she could still hear Piers's booming upper-class drawl.

'Ding-*dong*!' he said with a whistle. 'Who was that?'

She didn't wait to hear Mark's explanation of her existence, but scuttled away even faster—high heels permitting. The last thing she wanted to do was actually have to talk to people tonight. They would expect her to be dazzling and witty. And if she had ever been dazzling and witty in her previous life she had certainly forgotten by now. Socialising was something other people did. Even the prospect of a night down at the Anglers' Arms in Barkleigh filled her with fear and trembling. In comparison, this party was like purgatory with canapés.

A few dozen guests? Someone had underestimated a little.

The drawing room was like a *Who's Who* of popular music. Wasn't that…? You know, the guy who always seemed to be at number one? And that girl over there—Ellie had seen her latest music video only the other night on TV. Normal party nerves escalated into something far bigger and scarier. It would be really great if she could think of the girl's name—if she could recall *anyone's* name, actually. These were the sort of people who expected to be remembered.

She circled the drawing room, 'fluffing' the floral arrangements, hoping that no one talked to her and expected her to know who they were. But she wasn't really looking at what she was doing, and more leaves fell off due to her attention than she cared to notice. As soon as she could she slipped out and made her way to the kitchen.

CHAPTER FIVE

THERE was a strange calm to be had amidst the noise and movement of the kitchen. At least in here Ellie knew what she was doing. Her lists and charts were pinned to the cupboard doors, her timetable clung to the fridge door with the help of a few magnets, and waiters and waitresses were all jostling each other, doing exactly as they were supposed to.

It didn't take long before one of the catering company staff appeared with a question, and Ellie found herself busy for what seemed like a half an hour but turned out to be almost two hours. Eventually tiredness washed over her, the mind-fogging fatigue she knew she shouldn't ignore. Dodging dashing bodies and clattering trays suddenly became too much of an effort and she crept up the back staircase. Before she went to her room she carried on along the landing and looked over the banisters into the hall, where the party was still in full swing. She'd done well this evening, and she wanted one last mental picture of her achievement, to cement it firmly in her memory before she fled back to her bedroom and shut the door firmly behind her.

From her vantage point on the landing she watched the glittering crowd ebb and flow. The clink of champagne glasses and jumble of conversation drifted up from below. Surprisingly, she found the sound soothing now she was no longer in the thick of it.

Her eyes drifted here and there, searching. It wasn't until they fixed on Mark that she realised she'd been looking for him. He was the perfect host—she'd give him that. He was charming and smooth, always with a crowd around him. The group he was with laughed at something he said. So he was good company too, it seemed. But he didn't dominate the gathering, forcing people to look at him. They just flowed around him, accepting the good time he offered them.

That woman from the awards ceremony was talking to him now, batting her lashes and jutting her ample chest under his nose. Ellie rolled her eyes. And, funnily enough, when the woman turned to grab herself a cocktail from a passing tray, Mark did a microscopic version of the same expression. That made her smile. It also made her look a little closer.

He smiled. He talked. But every now and then he just drifted off and stared at nothing for a second, until the next excited guest drew him back into the conversation. It was almost as if…

No. That was a stupid idea. Why would someone throw a party if they didn't actually want to be at it themselves?

'What are you doing skulking up here? I've been looking for you everywhere.'

Ellie stopped breathing momentarily as Charlie appeared from nowhere.

'Don't do that!' Ellie whispered sharply, pressing her palm to her chest in an effort to slow her galloping heart. 'And I'm not skulking.'

Charlie stopped smiling and looked concerned. 'You're a bag of nerves,' she said, while giving Ellie's arm a reassuring rub. 'Come on, chill out. It is a party, after all…'

Ellie nodded. 'I know. But I need this to go well. I can't lose this job, Charlie, I can't—'

Without warning her eyes filled, and the party below glittered even harder than before.

'Hey!' Charlie's voice was gentle and her arm

rested around Ellie's shoulders, pulling her close. 'What's all this about?'

She took a deep breath. 'Did you tell him… Mark Wilder… about me?'

Charlie's three frown lines appeared above her nose. 'All I told him was that you were an old friend of mine and I thought you'd be perfect for the job. I wasn't lying, Ellie.'

Ellie scratched at a non-existent mark on the banister with a blunt fingernail. 'No. I mean, did you tell him about how I have problems with… about my…?'

Charlie's voice was low when she answered. 'No, I didn't tell him about the accident or how it's affected you. It's up to you whether you want to share that information with him.'

Okay, so Charlie had believed her when she'd sworn blind she had it in her to be a top-notch housekeeper. Now she just had to prove her right. Ellie's chest rose then fell deeply as she let out a huge breath. 'Right. Thank you.'

A soft look appeared on Charlie's face. 'Do you really think being here, moving away from home, will help you…you know…get over things?'

Suddenly Ellie needed to sit down. Her legs folded under her with the grace of a collapsing deckchair and she grabbed on to the banister with both hands. Charlie's arm appeared, firm and protective, around her shoulders.

'There's more to this sudden desire for a new job than just needing fresh scenery, isn't there, Ellie? Why did you really want to leave Barkleigh in such a hurry?'

Blast. Why did Charlotte Maxwell have to be so perceptive under her devil-may-care exterior? Ellie stared at the milling guests below. Their only problems were deciding which diamond to wear or which sports car to drive.

A feeling of loss washed over her, so deep, so overwhelming that she thought she might just dissolve into nothing right there on Mark Wilder's landing.

Sometimes she wished her brain would just finish the job and give up working all together. Then she could just evaporate. She'd be happy then, feeling nothing, remembering nothing. It was this half-in, half-out thing her memory did that was driving her to distraction.

'I can't go home,' she whispered. 'I just can't.'

'Why?'

'Remember Ginny? Chloe's godmother and my oldest friend?'

Charlie nodded. 'Yes, I remember her.'

Ellie didn't want to say it. Hearing the words spill out of her own mouth would remind her of everything she'd lost. Of everything she longed for.

'She's pregnant.'

She didn't look up. Couldn't.

Charlie's hand stopped stroking her arm and slid down over her wrist until their fingers meshed, Charlie's red fingernails bright against her pale skin. Ellie gripped her hand, hanging on to it as if it would anchor her.

'I know it's awful, but I think if I have to see her every day for the next eight months, seeing her grow bigger, seeing how happy she is with Steve, I might just go *properly* bonkers. I just had to get away.'

She was happy for Ginny and Steve, really she was, but how could she watch them add to their happy little family when her own had been wiped from the face of the earth? It was too...too... *blatant*.

Charlie didn't say anything, just hugged her tight. 'Do you want me to get you anything? A glass of water?'

Ellie shook her head. 'No. I'm just tired. I think I'll just stay here for a few seconds and then go to bed. You go on and enjoy the party.' She nodded to the hall below, where the rather good-looking man she'd seen Charlie with earlier was searching the crowd. 'I think someone's looking for you.'

Charlie smiled, and her eyes never left the man as he moved this way and that. 'If you're sure?' she said.

'I'm sure.' Ellie gave her a shove in the right direction and Charlie headed off down the stairs. The man spotted her, and the look he gave her as she descended was pure magic. Ellie sighed. At least someone was happy.

She moved a little further to the left, so she could see more of the hall. Mark was still leaning on the mantelpiece, and he had that distant look in his eyes again.

Her mind wandered back to his smile in the wedding photo. She'd seen him smile plenty of times tonight, but not one of those smiles had lit up his face like his smile for the woman in the wedding photo. Where was she now? What had happened? For the first time she realised there were scars beneath his good-humoured persona. From wounds that maybe hadn't fully healed. Her hand flew to the locket around her neck. She knew all about the pain those kinds of wounds could cause. As if he sensed she was watching him, Mark paused, his glass raised halfway to his lips. And then he turned his head and met her gaze. She froze. Could it be any more obvious she'd been staring at him and only him? She didn't think so.

Still, he didn't look cross. He wasn't smiling that irritating twinkly smile—wasn't mocking her. The other occupants of the room melted away, their conversation drowned out by a loud thudding sound.

Oh. That was her pulse.

Heat crept up her cheeks, but still she hadn't moved. And moving at this point would be a really good idea.

Still staring at Mark, she took a couple of wobbly steps backwards, then turned and fled along the corridor. For some reason she ignored her bedroom door and headed for the back staircase. She needed space, distance. And she didn't think she'd get that with only a ceiling and a couple of walls separating her from Mark Wilder.

The stupid stilettos strangled her ankles as she clattered down the back staircase. She paused at the bottom. No one was around, so she tiptoed down the corridor into the kitchen.

Ellie stole a smoked fish thing off a platter of canapés and popped it in her mouth. As she slid past a waitress carrying a tray of cocktails she pilfered one of those too, knocking it back and shuddering as whatever it was hit the back of her throat.

She edged past the round table near the French doors. An abandoned tray stood on the table, cluttered with champagne flutes, some empty, some full. She plucked one of the full ones and nipped out of her favourite escape route into the garden.

A wave of muffled laughter wafted past her on the clear night air. She took a sip of champagne, but barely tasted it. There was something she had to do first, before she could enjoy it properly.

Her feet were killing her.

She sat on a low stone wall and fiddled with the microscopic buckles. Pretty soon she'd flicked the shoes off and she hooked the satin straps under her fingers and headed into the garden.

The flagstones were cold and rough on the soles of her feet, and she veered in the direction of the lawn and sank her toes deep into it. Heaven! She closed her eyes and took another sip of champagne. The canapé was the first thing she had eaten all evening, and on an empty stomach it wasn't hard to feel the bubbles doing their work.

Funny how parties always sounded more inviting when you were on the outside. All she had wanted to do when she was in there was escape, yet now she was out here she felt strangely alone.

She took a few more steps on the springy grass, letting the blades invade the spaces between her toes. She wriggled them and drained the flute of its contents. Goosebumps flourished on her upper arms as she heard a low masculine voice behind her.

'Caught red-handed!'

A powerful pair of hands clamped down on Ellie's shoulders. The champagne glass slid out of her hand and bounced off her foot. She instinctively ducked down and forwards, wriggling out his grip, then swung round to face him.

He blinked groggily at her. 'What's the matter?' he slurred. 'Don't you like me?'

His name might have deserted her, but she hadn't forgotten this man. The floppy pale hair, the arrogant smirk. She didn't know who he was to Mark, but if the rest of his friends were like this, he could keep them.

He draped an arm across her shoulders. 'What d'you say we go for a little walk?'

She had to handle this carefully. He might be a pain in the behind, but he was Mark's guest too, so losing her temper would only get her in trouble. 'I'd rather not, thank you.'

His eyes were glassy and his breath reeked of whisky. She carefully peeled his arm off her shoulder. He lost his balance now he wasn't leaning on her for support, his feet sliding on the dewy grass. His smile faded.

'Hey! There's no need to be hoity-toity about it.'

'I didn't…I…' Oh, what was the use? He'd probably take any conversation as encouragement of some sort. The best thing to do was get out of here before she really did get *hoity-toity* with him.

She turned and walked back towards the house. He lumbered after her, stumbling slightly, and managed to grab hold of her arm and haul her towards him.

Something flashed white-hot inside her head. She dreaded these surges of anger, but could do very little to contain herself when they struck. She was going to blow, whether she liked it or not.

'Get off me!' she yelled.

He made a curious gurgle that she interpreted as a laugh, and clamped her to his chest. His lips made contact with the skin beneath her ear and slid down her neck in a slobbery trail.

'Ugh!'

Enough was enough. No more Miss Nice Guy. She swung Charlie's killer sandals wide and brought them crashing down on his temple.

* * *

Mark had suddenly had enough of standing around talking to the same people, having the same conversations he'd had last week. He needed fresh air.

Instinctively he headed for the kitchen, then paused at the threshold. Why had he come this way? He had the feeling he was looking for something but had forgotten what.

Nonsense, his conscience said. You know exactly why you're here...*who* you're looking for.

But it didn't matter. She wasn't there.

So he ducked past the busy catering staff and out of the French windows to the small lawn.

The floodlights on the outside of the house made the dark night even blacker, and it took him a few moments to realise he wasn't alone. A movement at the end of the lawn caught his eye and he made out two silhouettes. He almost grinned and shrugged it off as a couple of guests slipping away to get friendly, but something made him look again.

Piers was up to his old tricks, it seemed. He was a notorious flirt. The only reason Mark had invited him was because he needed his firm's specialist legal knowledge on a recording contract he was putting together. Still, Piers was relatively harmless, and most of the females in their circle of acquaintance knew how to deal with him. Mark peered deeper into the darkness. Just who was he with this time, anyway?

And then he was running, the sound of his own blood rushing and swirling in his ears. He worked out regularly enough, and his legs were pumping beneath him, but somehow he seemed to make torturous progress, like the slow-motion running in a dream.

The woman Piers was slobbering over was Ellie.

And there was no way he was going to let some jumped-up little twit who worked for his daddy's law firm foist himself on one of his staff. She might not know how to—

Mark almost slipped on the damp grass.

Perhaps she did.

He watched as Ellie gave Piers a first-class whack with her shoes. Piers stumbled and fell on the damp grass, clutching a hand to his head. Mark finally skidded to a halt in front of them and yanked Piers up by his collar. His right fist was itching to make contact with that pretty face. He ought to flatten him for treating Ellie that way.

'Mark, no!'

The panic in her voice was all he needed to make

him reconsider. He released the slimy runt and gave him a shove in the direction of the house.

'Go home, Piers. You're drunk.'

Piers wiped saliva from the edges of his mouth with the back of his hand.

'Steady on, Mark!'

He marched towards Piers and stopped inches from his face. Piers might have a reputation for being a ladies' man, but Mark had never suspected how nasty he could be with it. How could a man who appeared so polished during the working week turn out to be such a rat? Once again he'd believed the best in someone, only to be utterly disappointed.

'No. You *steady on*,' he said, with more than a hint of controlled fury in his voice. 'Don't ever set foot in this house again. In fact, don't bother to set foot in my offices again, either. As of Monday I will be seeking new legal representation—you and your firm are fired.'

Piers tugged at his tie and stood as tall as the whisky would let him.

'Now, look here. I could sue you for assault, manhandling me in that way!'

'Yes, you could. And I could tell the paparazzi hiding in my front bushes how you got plastered at my party and tried to grope one of my guests. I'm sure the partners at Blackthorn and Webb would welcome the publicity, don't you?'

Piers turned tail and lurched towards the house. Mark watched until he was out of sight, then faced Ellie. 'I'm so sorry about that. Are you all right?'

'Fine.' Her voice quivered enough to call her determined face a liar.

'You gave him one hell of a clout with those shoes!'

The shell-shocked expression gave way to a delightfully naughty smile. 'You should have warned him I was dangerous to mess with.'

The fingers of Mark's right hand wandered to the spot near his left collarbone, where she'd bitten him only a few weeks earlier. At the time he'd been livid, hadn't found it funny in the slightest. Tonight, however, he found he couldn't find it anything but, and he started to laugh.

To his surprise, Ellie joined him. Softly at first, with a giggle that hinted she was holding more of it in than she was letting out. But eventually she was laughing just as hard as he was, and the more he saw her eyes sparkle and her cheeks blush, the more he wanted to keep the moment going.

Look at her. When she smiled like that, lost the

glare and the frosty expression, she was… Not beautiful. At least not in the way Hollywood and the media defined the word. But he couldn't stop looking at her.

And why would he? She was laughing so hard she'd gone pink in the face and her eyes were squeezed shut. Any minute now he thought she'd keel over. It was adorable. Just as she threatened to make his prediction come true, she clutched at the air to steady herself. Her hand made contact with his upper arm and all the shared laughter suddenly died away.

Ellie looked away and tucked and escaped curl into the clip on top of her head. It bounced back again, unwilling to be leashed. His desire to reach forward and brush it away from her face was almost overpowering, but he'd done that so many times with other women. It would be too much of a cliché.

She looked up at him and shivered.

'You're cold.'

She started to protest, but he swung his jacket off and carefully hung it round her shoulders. It must be the night for clichés. This, too, was something he'd done more times than he could remember too—one of his *moves*, part of the game.

But it wasn't like that with Ellie. She'd been cold,

and he'd done something to remedy that. He wasn't playing any games. Mainly because he didn't know what the rules were with her. She made him feel different—unpolished, uncertain—as if he wasn't in control of whatever was going on.

He looked at the warm light spilling from Larkford's every window. He really ought to get back to his guests.

She moved slightly, and the friction of material between his fingers reminded him he was still holding the lapels of the jacket firmly. He really should let go. But Ellie was looking up at him, her eyes soft and unguarded, just as they had been when she'd stared down at him from the landing.

He'd liked that look then, and he liked it now. There wasn't a hint of greed or artifice in it. And that was a rare thing in his world. It was as if she saw something that surprised her, something that everyone else missed.

He'd seen her skirting the edge of the party, boredom clear on her face. And when he'd turned back to Melodie and the record producer he'd been chatting to he'd suddenly seen the whole gathering through Ellie's eyes, as if he'd been given X-ray specs that cut out the glare and the glitter, revealing everyone and everything for who and what they really were. Not much of what he'd seen would benefit from close scrutiny.

But out here on the lawn everything felt very real indeed. Uncomfortably so. His heart was hammering in his chest—and it wasn't from his race across the lawn.

She was tantalisingly close, her feelings clearly written in her face, floating across the surface. He felt her warm breath on his neck, sending shivers to the roots of his hair. He clenched the lapels of the dinner jacket, pulling her closer until only a molecule of air prevented their faces from touching. Normally he'd go in for the kill now, take the advantage while he had it, but he waited.

What for, he wasn't exactly sure.

The world seemed to shrink into the tiny space between his lips and hers. At least Ellie was aware of nothing but this, nothing beyond it. And, since remembering past or future was a struggle sometimes anyway, she finally let go and just existed in the moment. This particular moment revolved around a choice, one that was hers alone: to flow with the moment or push against it.

She was so tired of fighting herself, tired of pushing herself, of always keeping everything under constant surveillance. Just once she wanted to follow an impulse rather than resist it.

She wanted *this*.

Hesitantly, she pressed her lips against his, splaying her hands across his chest to steady herself. For a moment he did nothing, and her heart plummeted, but then he pulled her to him, sliding his hands under his suit jacket to circle her waist, and kissed her back.

All those women who fluttered and twittered merely at the sight of him would have melted clean away if they'd been on the receiving end of a kiss like this. Every mad hormonal urge she'd been fighting for the last few weeks roared into life and she didn't resist a single one.

It was a kiss of need, exploration…perfection.

She didn't need to think, to struggle to remember anything. And she wouldn't have been able to if she'd tried, not with Mark's teeth nipping at her lower lip, his hands sliding up her back until they brushed the bare flesh of her shoulders. Ellie reached up to feel the faint stubble on his jaw with her fingertips. He groaned and pulled her close enough to feel the muscles in his chest flexing as his arms moved. She let her head drop back when his lips pressed against the tingling skin just below her jaw, and she slid her fingers round the back of his head, running them through the short hair there and feeling him shiver.

A tray clanged inside the kitchen, and the noise cut cleanly and smoothly through the night air. They both froze, and the moment they'd shared shattered along with the glasses landing on the kitchen floor.

There was a horrible sense of *déjà vu* as they stared at each other, neither sure of what was going on and what they should do next.

Mark grasped for words inside his head. *Say something!*

He reached for her. 'Ellie…'

Come on, smooth talker! Where's all your patter now?

She stared back at him, wide-eyed and breathless. Then, before he could get his thoughts collected into syllables, she bolted into the house.

See? Unpredictable. He couldn't have guessed she was going to do that. After all, it wasn't the normal response he got when he kissed a woman—quite the reverse.

He raced after her and burst through the French windows into the kitchen. Precious seconds were lost as he collided with a fully laden waiter. The clattering of trays and muttered apologies masked the sound of her bare feet slapping on the tiles as she tore out of the kitchen and down the passageway that led to the back stairs.

He dodged another waiter and ran after her, only to be corralled by a group of guests.

'Mark!'

He turned to find Kat, looking all dishevelled and misty. Her puppy-dog eyes pleaded with him.

'It's Razor…'

She sniffed, and a single tear rolled down her cheek. Mark looked hopelessly at the staircase to his left, then at Kat, and back to the staircase. Kat hung on to his sleeve. He knew her well enough by now to realise that full meltdown was only seconds away. He put his own desires on the back burner and guided her through the crush in the drawing room to his study.

The boy wonder had undoubtedly been his usual considerate self, and Mark's shoulder was the one designated for crying on these days. He'd resisted that in the beginning, but he was too much of a sucker for a forlorn female to just pat Kat on the head and say, *There, there.*

As he ushered her into the study and shut the door he reasoned to himself that Ellie wasn't going anywhere for the moment. It would probably be better to give her a few minutes before he went after her—some thinking time. So he allowed Kat to spill out the whole sorry story and soak his shirt with her tears.

Ellie sat in the dark, shivering despite the central heating. She couldn't bear to turn on the light and see Sam's picture on the bedside table. Her eyes were sticky with tears and her nose was running. With a loud sniff she toppled back onto the mattress and curled into a ball.

'What was I thinking?'

Oh, but *thinking* hadn't been the problem. It was what she'd *done* that had messed everything up. Thoughts were fleeting, easily lost, erased or misplaced. Actions, however, were a little more concrete. And in this case definitely more memorable.

Just the memory of Mark's lips on hers was enough to make her flush hot and cold again.

How could she have done this to Sam? Wonderful, loving, dependable Sam? She was sure he would have been happy to think she would find someone else and rebuild her shattered life, but Mark Wilder! He was the worst kind of womaniser there was.

She searched the darkness above her head for an answer, desperate to make sense of it all.

But Mark hadn't seemed like a womaniser tonight in the garden, quite the reverse. He'd sent Piers Double-Barrelled packing, backing her up and taking her side, and he hadn't even taken advantage of the situation when she'd been vulnerable and heaving with hormones. She could have walked away…

Maybe it wasn't about Mark. Maybe it was a symptom of her decision to break free, to learn to live again. Perhaps part of herself that she'd thought had died and been buried along with Sam had sprung to life again. She was a young woman still. It was just a healthy interest in the opposite sex, a natural response to a good-looking man.

But that train of thought derailed just as fast as the last one had.

It was only since meeting Mark that she'd been anything but numb. He was a catalyst of some kind. And…and if it was just about pent-up desires, she wouldn't have rejected Piers. He was suave and attractive, but it didn't stop her experiencing a wave of revulsion every time she thought of him.

So she was back to Mark. Her brain was swinging in wild arcs, but it always came back to

Mark. What was she going to do about that... about *him*?

His attraction to her was genuine, there was no mistaking that, but it wouldn't last. Men like him didn't stay with women like her. After a couple of months it would fizzle out and she'd be left alone again. And in search of a new job.

She didn't want an affair, or a fling, or a one-night stand. Settling for less than the all-encompassing love she'd had for Sam seemed like being unfaithful to his memory. It would be like losing the Crown Jewels and replacing them with paste and nickel that made your skin turn green. This thing with Mark, whatever it was, it couldn't go anywhere. It couldn't be anything.

She sniffed again and stretched out a little. Why? Why be interested in someone like him? She could say it was the money, or the success, his looks and his charm, but it wasn't any of those things. Tonight she'd glimpsed something else behind the cheeky, boyish charm. Something darker and deeper that resonated with a similar *something* inside her too.

A faint hint of Mark's aftershave drifted into her nostrils. She looked up, half expecting to see him standing there, waiting for her, but the room was empty. Then she realised she was still wearing his jacket. His masculine scent clung to it, and she was reminded of the moment he'd put it on her in the garden.

He'd seemed so vulnerable standing there. For a man who had women drop at his feet on a daily basis he'd almost seemed unsure of himself. Not at all what she'd expected.

She whimpered and covered her face with her hands, even though there was no one there to see her blush.

How was she going to face him in the morning?

CHAPTER SIX

MARK stumbled downstairs some time after ten. He'd intended to get up earlier, but he hadn't dropped off until dawn and then his sleep had been heavy, full of dreams where he was running from unseen predators. He'd wanted to be fresh and calm this morning, to deal with the aftermath of last night's events with just a little panache.

He didn't have to search hard for Ellie, though; he could smell something delicious wafting from the kitchen, and he followed the mouthwatering smell like a zombie.

Well, almost like a zombie. His heart rate was pattering along too fast for him to be considered officially dead. Was he...was he *nervous*?

He'd spent hours last night in his study, going over and over it all in his head. Not that he'd come to any earth-shattering conclusions. He had a housekeeper. She kissed like a dream. That was about the sum total of it.

All he'd done was kiss her. It was hardly a big deal.

All he'd done... He should listen to himself.

If it had just been a kiss, his heart wouldn't be flapping around inside his chest like a fish out of water.

He liked Ellie. And not in the let's-have-dinner-at-the-Ivy kind of way he normally liked women. It felt different. As if this kind of *liking* had a different shape, was a different kind of entity all together.

Now, that was a scary thought.

Like Helena, Ellie was one of those delicate beings, beautiful in their frailty like an orchid or a butterfly. And that made her even more dangerous. He knew he couldn't resist getting drawn in by women like that, finding himself wanting to protect them, to care for them until they were whole again. It was a weakness, he knew, but one that he channelled into his clients these days, by being the best manager in the business. At least they paid him for his devotion.

That kind of woman sucked everything out of a man until he had nothing left to give. And then she took what he'd done, all the tender, loving care he'd given, and bestowed it on someone else, someone who didn't remind her of the pain.

Someone who didn't remind her of who she used to be when she was just a shell, empty and hurting.

He couldn't do that again. He couldn't be that for anyone again.

So he would just have to deflect Ellie, dazzle her, and move things back to where they should be— on a purely professional level.

If he could talk a highly strung diva down from demanding three-hundred-pound-a-bottle mineral water that had been blessed by a Tibetan priest in her dressing room, he could surely manage this. And then he would invent a reason to go and stay at his flat in London for a few days. It wasn't running away; it was self-preservation.

'Morning,' he said, overcompensating a little and sounding much too relaxed as he entered the kitchen. Ellie had her back turned to him. She was stirring something in a saucepan on the hob and returned his greeting in a cool, clipped voice, not looking up from the pan.

'What are you doing?'

Ah, yes. This is the smooth wit and banter you are famous for... This will charm the socks off her and sort everything out.

Ellie didn't say anything, just stirred harder.

'It smells great. What is it?'

'I decided to make a big batch of bolognaise and freeze it in smaller portions for quick suppers,' she said in a starchy voice. 'Would you like me to stop and fetch you breakfast?'

That was the last thing he wanted. Far too awkward.

'It's okay. I'm more than capable of getting my own coffee.'

He grabbed himself a mug of coffee and sat down at the circular wooden table near the French windows that led to the garden. Ellie was pushing what he now recognised as beef mince round the pan with a wooden spoon. It spat and hissed, the only sound in the rapidly thickening atmosphere.

He cleared his throat. 'Ellie, listen…'

'Look, Mark, I know where this is going.'

'You do?' He rubbed his nose with the heel of his hand.

'I do. And let's not go there.'

Good. They were reading off the same page. Why, then, had his stomach bottomed out like a plummeting lift?

'Okay,' he said, not trusting himself with anything more complicated. It seemed as if Ellie was doing fine on her own, anyway. She took a deep breath in readiness for another speech.

'You're my boss. You spend your time flitting around the globe and living the high life. And I'm…' She looked at the ceiling, searching for the right word.

'I know I'm your boss—of course I know that—and you're…'

Surprising? Appealing? Unforgettable? Those were the words that filled his head. None of them were the right ones to come out of his mouth, though.

'You're…'

Ellie's gaze wandered down from the heavens and settled on him. 'I'm your *housekeeper*.'

'Right.' That was correct. But it didn't *feel* like the right answer.

She shook her head, her curls bouncing slightly. 'To be honest, you and me, it's just—'

'Complicated?'

She shrugged one shoulder. 'I was going for tacky or predictable, but your word works too.'

Ouch.

'I'm your employee, and I think we should keep our relationship on a professional basis,' she said, turning to face him fully.

'I agree with you one hundred percent.'

He looked hard at her, trying to work out what she

was thinking. Her words were telling him she was fine, but her tone said something entirely different.

'You seem upset…'

She waved the wooden spoon in dismissal.

'Upset? I'm not upset!'

'Good.'

She gave him a blatantly fake smile, and returned her attention to the meat in the pan.

'Annoyed, then?'

More frantic stirring.

'Nope. Not at all.' She started jabbing the wooden spoon at the remaining lumps.

Ellie might be different from a lot of women he knew in a lot of ways, but the whole pretending to be fine when she clearly was not was horribly familiar.

'Ellie, I know I may have been a bit impulsive last night, but I don't think we…*I* did anything wrong.'

'Oh, you don't?' she said through clenched teeth.

'No. Do you?'

Now he was totally lost. Why did women have this secret agenda that read like code to normal human beings—men, in other words?

The pan spat ferociously as Ellie added a jar of tomatoey gloopy stuff and mixed it in. She turned to face him and took a step away from the counter, still holding the dripping spoon.

'You're unbelievable, do you know that? You live in a lovely little Mark bubble where everything is perfect. You haven't got a clue what real life is like!'

He thought he did a pretty good job of living life, thank you very much, and he didn't much care for someone he hardly knew judging him for it.

'I don't?'

'No! You don't. Real people have real feelings, and you can't just go messing around with them. You live in this rarefied world where you do whatever you want, get whatever you want and everything goes right for you. Not everybody has that luxury. And you waste it, you know? You really do.'

Something in her stare made him hold back the smart retort poised on his lips. Through the film of tears gathering in her eyes he saw determination and an honesty that was surprising—and not a little unnerving.

Something was very wrong, but as usual he was totally mystified as to what was going on inside her head. Why was she blaming him? He hadn't been the one to start it last night. *She* had kissed him, remember? And he certainly hadn't meant to mess around with her feelings, but perhaps he had…without realising it.

Maybe he *was* clueless. He needed to consider her accusation a little more fully before he gave a real answer.

Ellie made use of the silence to ram her point home. 'I think it's best for both of us if we just put that…you know, the…'

A crack in her anger showed as she desperately tried to avoid using the word 'kiss'. It would have been funny if she hadn't been giving him the brush-off.

'Let's just put what happened last night down to champagne and temporary insanity, okay? I don't want to lose this job.'

He nodded just once. 'And I need to start looking for a new housekeeper like I need a hole in the head.'

Finally she breathed out and her shoulders relaxed a little. 'I'm glad we understand each other,' she said with a small jut of her chin, and turned her attention back to the bolognaise sauce.

She was right. He knew she was right. It was just…

Aw, forget it. He'd spent the last decade fooling everyone—even himself—that he was 'living the dream'. He might just as well return to that happy, alpha-wave state and forget that he'd ever yearned for anything more.

If you can, a little voice whispered in his ear. *If you can...*

Mark disappeared back to London the next day, much to Ellie's relief. But it didn't stop him coming back to Larkford again the following weekend. Or the one after that. During the week she could relax, enjoy her surroundings, but the weekends were something else. Stiff. Awkward. And, although she'd never expected anything more than a professional relationship with the man, now they were operating on that level it just seemed, well...weird.

And that was how it continued for the next month or so.

So, there she was on a Saturday afternoon, hiding out in the kitchen, preparing the evening meal, even though she needn't start for hours yet. But it was good to keep herself busy and out of a certain person's way. Not that it had been hard today. He might be at home, but he was obviously working; he'd hardly left the study all day. They were keeping to their separate territories as boxers did their corners of the ring.

She was still cross with herself for being too weak to control her brain's fried electrical signals. They still all short-circuited every time he appeared. It was as if her neurons had rewired themselves with a specialised radar that picked up only him as he breezed around the house, as calm as you like, while her fingernails were bitten so low she'd practically reached her knuckles.

Blip. Blip. Blip.

There it went again. Her core temperature rose a couple of notches. He was on the move; she just knew it. She stopped chopping an onion and listened. After about ten seconds she heard what she'd been waiting for—footsteps in the hall, getting louder.

She kept her eyes on her work as Mark entered the kitchen. The coffee machine sputtered. Liquid sloshed into a cup. The rubber heel of a stool squeaked on the floor. Silence. The tiny hairs on the back of her neck bristled.

Just carry on as if he's not there.

The knife came down hard on the chopping board—thunk, thunk, thunk—so close she almost trimmed her non-existent nails. She threw the onion pieces into a hot frying pan where they hissed back at her. According to the recipe they should be finely chopped. The asymmetrical lumps looked more like the shapes Chloe had produced as a toddler when left to her own devices with paper and safety scissors.

She sliced the next onion with exaggerated care and flipped the switch for the extractor hood above the hob. It was too still in the kitchen. Too hot. She plucked a papery clove of garlic from a nearby pot.

Only one more left.

That gave her an idea, stunning in its simplicity. She turned to face Mark with what she hoped was a cool stare. He sat looking straight back at her, waiting.

'I need to go out—to get some things I can't find at the local shops from the big supermarket. Is there anything you'd like me to get you that's not on the shopping list?' She nodded to indicate a long pad hanging on a nail where she always listed store cupboard items as soon as they'd run out. She even managed a smile on the last few words, so delighted was she at the thought of getting out of the house and into fresh, uncomplicated air.

He just lifted his shoulders and let them drop again. 'Nope. Nothing in particular.'

Most housekeepers would be glad of having a boss with such an easygoing nature, but the contrast with her own jangled emotions just made her want to club him over the head with his large wooden pepper mill. She strode to the other side of the room and snatched her handbag from where it hung on the back of a chair.

It wasn't more than a minute later that she was sitting in the driver's seat of her car, turning the key in the ignition.

Nothing.

'Come on, old girl!' she crooned, rubbing the dashboard. 'Don't let me down now. You are my ticket out of here—at least for the afternoon.' She tried again, pumping her foot frantically on the pedal. Her old banger coughed, threatening to fire up, then thought better of it. She slapped the steering wheel with the flat of her hands.

'Traitor.'

She collected her bag and strutted back into the kitchen, chin in the air. Mark was still sitting on the stool, finishing his coffee.

'Problems?'

'Car won't start. I'll have to go another day, after I've had the old heap looked at.'

Mark stood up and pulled a bunch of keys from his pocket. 'Come on, then.'

'What?'

'I'll take you.'

'No, it's okay. Honestly. You're busy.'

'No problem,' he said with that lazy grin of his, the one straight out of a toothpaste ad. 'I could do with getting away from my desk and letting things settle in my head, anyway.'

Ellie groaned inwardly. Now the afternoon was going to be torture rather than escape. She followed him reluctantly to his car. It was a sleek, gunmetal-grey Aston Martin. She could almost see his chest puff out in pride as he held the passenger door open for her.

Boys and their toys. What was the theory about men with flash cars?

Mark didn't need to take his eyes off the road to know that Ellie had shifted position and was now staring out of the window. He was aware of every sigh, every fidget. And her body language was yelling at him in no uncertain terms—*back off*!

What if she'd been right all those weeks ago when she'd shouted at him? He'd given the whole thing a lot of thought. Did he live in a 'Mark bubble'? A self-absorbed little universe where he was the sun and all revolved around him? Did he now waltz through life—well, relationships— without a backward glance?

If he did, it hadn't always been that way. His thoughts slid inevitably to Helena. That woman had a lot to answer for. He'd have stayed by her side until his dying day. Hadn't he promised as much, dressed in a morning suit in front of hundreds of witnesses? Stupidly, he'd thought she'd felt the same way, but it turned out that he'd confused *loyalty* with *neediness*. She'd stuck around while he'd been useful and then, when he'd needed her to be the strong one for a change, she'd walked away.

And he hadn't seen it coming. Before the news had broken, he'd been thinking to himself that Helena had finally reached a place where she seemed less troubled, and he'd even been thinking about broaching the subject of having kids.

But then his first management company had gone belly-up because he'd made the same mistake with Nuclear Hamster. He'd really believed in them, had remortgaged his house, emptied his savings accounts to give them a start in the business. Friends had warned him not to take a cut of the net profit in their first contract when most managers took a percentage of the gross. The album had sold well, but on tour they'd run up huge bills—having parties, chartering private jets—and at the end of the day fifteen percent of no profit whatsoever and creditors knocking at the door meant he'd had to declare himself bankrupt. It hadn't been any comfort at all to know he'd walked into a trap of his own making because he made the mistake of trusting people he'd got close to.

He'd thought Helena's coolness, her distance, had been because she'd been worried about money. Heck, he'd been terrified himself. He'd known how expensive it was to take a rock band to court. But what else could he have done? He couldn't have let one bunch of freeloaders ruin his career and reputation, could he?

All at once the love and care she'd demanded from him for the previous four years had been deemed suffocating, and without the nice lifestyle there hadn't been much incentive to stick around. Helena had declared she needed space, that it was time to stand on her own two feet. You name the cliché and she'd flung it at him.

Of course that hadn't lasted more than two minutes. She'd soon found herself a rich TV executive to pander to her needs and the whole cycle had started all over again. Oh, she'd sniffed around again when he'd won his court case and rebuilt his company, but he hadn't even returned her calls. If she couldn't stand by him through the tough times—through living in a bedsit and eating beans on toast for months, through losing all his so-called friends and business associates—then she didn't deserve even a minute of his attention. He'd surprised himself at his own hardness.

And it gave him a grim sense of satisfaction to know she'd burned her bridges too soon. Half a ton of debts was all she'd been entitled to in the divorce proceedings. If she'd waited a couple of years before she'd bailed she would have done a lot better for herself.

Light drizzle peppered the windscreen. He watched it build into a pattern of dots. A flick of a switch round the steering wheel created a blank canvas where a new and completely different design was free to form.

He turned off the main road into a narrow country lane and determined to concentrate on the road in front of him. The Aston Martin was heaven to drive. Normally he didn't have time to sit back and enjoy it, always hurrying from A to B, always focusing on the destination instead of the journey. Ellie's presence as his passenger made him want to savour the experience.

The trip to the supermarket had been fun, in a

way. Spending time with her on neutral territory had been different. She'd relaxed a little. He felt strangely comfortable pushing the trolley along behind her as she'd browsed the aisles, squeezing avocados and reading the backs of packets. Of course he'd had no idea what she was doing half the time, or what she'd make with the assortment of ingredients she'd flung in the trolley, but the fact *she* knew gave her an air of wisdom.

The raindrops on the windscreen got fatter and rounder. They were going to have to get a move on if they were going to get home before it tipped down. The purr of the engine seduced him into going faster. He was pretty confident in his driving skills and was starting to become familiar with these lanes, anticipating the sweep and curve of the overgrown hedgerows as they got closer to Larkford. He glanced at Ellie. She was staring straight ahead, a grim look on her face.

He swung round a corner into a flat, fairly straight stretch of road and picked up speed. He loved the growl of satisfaction as the engine worked harder. It responded with eagerness to every nudge on the accelerator.

The sky darkened and the wild hedgerows whipped past, clawing at the car as if they were jealous. Inside the low-slung sports car the air was full of static. He could almost feel the crackles arcing from Ellie's thigh as he changed gear, his knuckles threatening to stroke the warm denim of her jeans.

A pheasant burst from the hedge in a flurry of feathers. He heard Ellie's sharp intake of breath, and out of the corner of his eye saw her grip the edge of her seat. After he'd braked slightly, he turned his head fully towards her, meaning to reassure her.

'Mark…' The trembling plea hardly escaped her lips.

'It's okay. We weren't going to—'

'Mark…please…!'

The urgency in her voice panicked him. Her face was frozen in stark horror. He looked back down the lane and his stomach lurched as he saw the farm vehicle pulling out of a concealed entrance. He squeezed the brake harder, slowing to a smooth crawl, and allowed the rust-speckled tractor to rumble past them. He pulled away and silently congratulated himself on not even leaving a skid mark on the tarmac.

'Stop the car.' Her voice was faint, but determined.

'But we're almost home.'

Her voice came in breathy gasps. 'I said…stop the car…I want to get out.'

Mark's faced creased into a scowl of disbelief as Ellie scrabbled at the door lever, desperate to free the lock. He pulled deftly into a passing place. Before the car had fully stopped Ellie had popped her seat belt and staggered out of the car, stumbling forward, gulping in damp country air. She was shaking, her whole body quivering.

Mark sat paralysed in the driver's seat, too stunned to move. Then, coming to his senses, he unbuckled himself and ran after her. It didn't take long to catch her as she straggled up the lane, half in a dream state.

He grabbed her wrist and pulled her firmly to him. Her head lodged just under his chin, and for a split second she moulded against him before pushing him away again.

He should have remembered she was surprisingly strong for a woman so soft and rounded-looking. He managed to grab one of her wrists before she darted off again down the middle of the road.

She turned to face him, fury in her eyes. 'I asked you to *stop* the car!'

Her free arm waved around wildly and she pulled and tugged the other, trying to twist it out of his grasp.

Mark stared at her. What on earth was wrong

with her? Why such angst over a stupid tractor? Puzzled as he was, he held on to her as gently as he could without letting her run down the lane into oncoming traffic. Ellie swung towards the middle of the road as she attempted to wrench her arm away from him again, all the while pressing a flattened palm to her chest and breathing in shallow gasps.

The nasal blast of a horn pierced the air and Mark grabbed her back out of the path of an approaching car. He stumbled backwards with her until his feet were on the grassy verge, the gnarled twigs of the ancient hedgerow piercing his back.

Ellie's mouth worked against his chest. He could feel her jaw moving, feel the moist warmth of her breath through his pullover. She might have been trying to shout at him, but nothing remotely resembling a word was included in the few noises tumbling out of her mouth. Her tiny hands balled into fists and she punched him on the chest. Twice.

He might not know what was going on here— clueless, as always—but one thing was certain: whether she knew it or not, Ellie needed him in this moment. She needed someone to be angry with, someone to fall apart on. And, hey, wasn't he the most likely candidate to light her fuse at the moment, anyway? He might as well take the brunt of whatever this was.

No way was he about to brush this situation off with a joke. It was time to face the challenge he'd walked away from so many times over the last decade. No amount of sequins or cash would defuse the situation. He was just going to have to be 'real' too. He hoped to God he still had it in him.

She was still trying to push away from him, but now the tears came. She gulped and cried and sobbed as if she'd never stop. He swallowed rising fear at such intense emotion, whispered words of comfort in her ear and waited for the squall to wear itself out. Eventually the sobbing became shallower and she surrendered to it, burying her face in his jumper. All those crying sessions with Kat now just seemed like practice sessions leading up to this moment—and he was thoroughly glad of the training.

How he wished he could do something to ease her pain. It was so raw. Perhaps if he held her long enough, tight enough, something of him she needed would seep through the damp layers between them in a kind of osmosis. He wanted to make up the missing parts of her. Loan her his uncanny ability to shield himself from everything, to feel nothing he didn't want to.

His fingers stilled in her curls as he thought what a poor exchange it would be. He had nothing to give her, really. She could teach him so much more. Her determination, her ability to say what she felt whether she wanted to or not. She knew how to live, while he only knew how to dazzle.

The sky turned to lavender-grey as afternoon retreated. Mark let the thump of his heart beat away the minutes as Ellie became motionless against him, pulling in deep breaths. She peeled her face from his chest, the ridge marks of the wool knit embedded on her hot cheek, half blinded by the thick tears clogging her eyelashes. Mark held her face tenderly in his palms and looked deep into her pink-rimmed eyes, desperate to soothe away the tempest he didn't understand.

Ellie stared back at him.

He could see weariness, despair, the ragged depths of her soul, but also a glimmer of something else. Her eyes were pleading with him, asking him to give her hope.

His voice was soft and low. 'Tell me.'

It was not a demand, but a request. Ellie's lips quivered and a tear splashed onto his hand. Never taking his gaze from her, he led her to the passenger door and sat her on the edge of the leather seat, crouching to stay on her level, keeping her hands tight between his.

Ellie let out a shuddering sigh as she closed her eyes. Her top lip tucked under her bottom teeth. He could see she was searching for words. Her pale green eyes flipped open and looked straight into his.

Her voice was low and husky from crying. 'It was just a panic attack. I get them sometimes… Sorry.'

He wasn't sure he was buying this. A forgotten voice inside his head—his conscience, maybe?—poked and prodded him and dared him not to let this slide. Whatever she needed to say was important. And it was important she said it now. So he did the only thing he could do. He waited.

For a few minutes no one spoke, no one moved, and then she dipped her head and spoke in a low, hoarse voice. 'My husband and daughter were killed in a car accident on a wet day like this,' she said, looking down at their intertwined fingers.

'I'm so sorry.'

Well, that was probably the most inadequate sentence he'd ever uttered in his life, but it was all he could come up with. Lame or not, it was the truth. He was sorry for her. Sorry for the lives that had been cut off too early. Sorry he hadn't even known she'd been married. He squeezed her hands tighter.

'It was almost four years ago now. We were driving home from a day out shopping. I'd bought Chloe a pair of sparkly pink party shoes. She never even got to wear them…'

There was nothing he could say. Nothing he could do but let her talk.

'The police said it was joyriders. They'd been daring each other to go faster and faster… There was a head-on collision at a sharp bend on a country lane. Nobody could stop in time—the road was too wet.'

How awful. Such a tragedy. He wondered how she'd found out. Had the police come knocking at her door? A word she'd muttered earlier came back to haunt him.

We?

He rubbed the back of her hand with his thumb. 'You were in the car too?'

She sniffed and hiccupped at the same time, then looked at him, a deep gnawing ache in her eyes. 'I was driving.'

Mark pulled her back into his arms. He could feel her salty tears on his own cheek, smell her shampoo as she laid her head on his shoulder. He closed his eyes and drank in her gentle fragrance. Her soft ringlets cushioned his face, a corkscrew curl tickling his nose.

'Feel,' she said. At first he didn't understand, but she pulled his hand away from her back and placed it on the right side of her head. Where there should have been smooth bone beneath skin and hair there was a deep groove in her scalp. Mark stroked the hair there too. Gently. So gently.

'The police told me there wasn't anything I could have done,' she said quietly. 'But I don't remember. And it's like having a huge question mark hanging over my life. I'm never going to know that for sure. What if I could have reacted a split second faster or turned the wheel another way?'

She drifted off into silence again.

His voice left him. He'd never imagined…

And he realised how stupid he'd been now. He should have curbed the adolescent urge to show off around her, racing his car down the winding lanes. All this was his fault.

Ellie sighed and relaxed into him. It felt perfect, as if she'd been carved to fit there. In recent weeks he'd not been able to stop himself fantasising about holding her close like this, kissing her brow, her nose, her lips. Well, not exactly like this. But he knew if he gave in to the fierce pull of his own desire now he would desecrate the moment, and he knew it would never come again.

She stirred, pulling back from him slightly to drag her hands across her face in an effort to mop up the congealed tears.

'I'm sorry.' Her voice was so faint it was barely a whisper.

'No. *I'm* sorry. For starting all this in the first place…'

'You couldn't have known.' All the fizzing, spitting irritation she'd held in her eyes every time she'd looked at him since the night of the party was gone.

'Well, I know now. And I am sorry. For anything—everything—I did to upset you. You must know I would never do that on purpose, however much of an idiot I may seem sometimes.'

Her mouth curved imperceptibly and her eyes never left his. He felt a banging in his chest just as hard as when she'd been thumping on it with her fist. He stood up and rested his hand on the door to steady himself.

'Let's go home.'

CHAPTER SEVEN

NO LIGHTS were on in the drawing room. The fire-light flickered, playing with the shadows on the wall. Mark sat in his favourite chair and savoured the aromatic warmth of his favourite whisky as it smouldered in his throat. The only sounds were the cracking of the wood on the fire and the laborious ticking of the antique clock in the corner. Ellie had gone to bed early, and he was left to relentlessly mull over the events of the afternoon.

They had driven back to Larkford in complete silence, but it had been different from the combustible atmosphere of their outward journey. The calm after the storm. He hadn't wanted to jinx the easy comfort by opening his big mouth. He hadn't been sure if Ellie was lost in the recent past, or plumbing the depths of earlier memories, and it hadn't felt right to ask.

The vivid evening sky had deepened to a velvety indigo by the time they'd drawn up in front of the house. Mark had carried the shopping in, forbidding Ellie to help, and had suggested she have a long hot bath. He'd realised, as he'd struggled with the dilemma of where to put the dried pasta they'd just bought, that he didn't have a clue where stuff went in his own kitchen. He'd got down to a short-list of two possible cupboards when he'd heard the unmistakable sound of Ellie's bare feet on the tiles.

'Top left,' she said quietly.

'Thanks,' he replied, shutting the cupboard door he was holding open and walking to another one on the other side of the room. When he put the linguine away next to the other bags of pasta he turned to look at her. She was dressed in a ratty pink towelling robe that was slightly longer at one side than the other. Her hair was wet, the blonde curls darkened and subdued, but struggling to bounce back. Her face was pink and scrubbed, eyes bright. He had never seen her look so gorgeous.

She walked towards him. His heart thumped so loudly in his chest he thought she was bound to hear it. But she didn't stop and stare at him. She didn't laugh. Instead, she was smiling, eyes hesitant but warm. He was hypnotised.

'Thank you, Mark. For everything.'

She was only a foot away from him now, and she

stood on tiptoes and placed an exquisitely delicate kiss on his cheek.

'Goodnight,' she said gently, and she headed for the door.

'Night,' he replied absently, still feeling the sweet sting of her lips on his cheek.

Now, hours later, he could still feel the tingle of that kiss. He took another sip of the whisky and rubbed the spot with the tips of his fingers.

At least he understood that tragic look in her eyes now. Ellie was haunted; the ghosts of her lost family still followed her. She had lived through more hurt than he could possibly imagine and yet she had found the strength to carry on living.

He looked back at his own life over the last decade and berated himself for his self-centredness and cowardice. He'd been afraid to let anyone close because he'd allowed one gold-digging woman to discolour his view of the rest of her sex. Instead of moving on and growing from the experience he'd sulked and cut himself off from any possibility of being hurt again, learning to cauterise the wounds with sarcastic humour and a don't-care attitude. He'd taken the easy way out.

Not like Ellie. She was brave. How did you pick

yourself up again and keep on living after something like that?

He downed the rest of the whisky and sat for a long time, holding the empty glass. Once upon a time he'd written her off as fragile, but she was possibly the strongest person he'd ever met.

Be careful what you wish for, Ellie thought, as she exited the kitchen through the French windows and took her usual route round the garden. All those months in Barkleigh, longing for breathing space, the chance to be on her own without anyone fussing…

Well, now she had air and space in bucketloads. And for a while it had been good, and she thought she'd escaped that creeping sense of loneliness that had seeped into her bones at the cottage, but it had just followed her here.

Okay, most of the time it was pretty perfect. Like now, when the early-morning sun was gently warming her skin as she wandered a subconscious route round the gardens, her habitual cup of tea cradled in her upturned hands, but sometimes all this room, this space, it was a little…well…

She shook her head. She was just being silly.

It was hardly surprising she was finding life a

little solitary. Only a couple of days after the disastrous trip to the supermarket Mark had disappeared, mumbling something about putting a big deal together, and she hadn't seen him for more than a fortnight. She guessed he was staying up at his flat in London, going to meetings all day. She tried not to speculate on what he might get up to at night.

The view of the Thames from his flat must be stunning, the vibe of the warm summer nights exciting, but if she had a choice of living in a crowded city, full of exhaust fumes and scary commuters, and being here at Larkford, she knew what she'd pick.

She kicked her flip-flops off as she reached the edge of the lawn and sighed in pleasure as the soles of her feet met soft grass that was dry, but still cool from the early-morning dew.

It was silly, but she couldn't shake the feeling that Mark was staying away deliberately. Maybe he was embarrassed. He wouldn't be the first person not to be able to handle her unique circumstances. She'd tried to run away from that feeling too, hadn't she? And now it had tracked her down and turned up on her doorstep.

She looked around the garden. The roses on the wrought-iron arches that lined the main path were in flower, a variety with frilly shell-pink petals. The smell was fantastic.

She sighed. Well, if Mark wanted to stay away, she couldn't stop him. It just seemed such a pity he was missing how beautiful his home looked. Every day there was something new to admire in the garden, another flower opening its buds or shooting out new green leaves. Maybe Mark wasn't the sort of person to notice these kind of things, but even if you didn't notice the details you couldn't help but feel rested here.

When she went back inside the house and checked her laptop she found an e-mail from Mark, and this time, instead of giving another boring, bland reply, she decided to add a little bit about Larkford—about the rose walk and how the wisteria on the back of the house was fairly dripping with flowers, how the hazy summer mornings burnt off into hot, bright afternoons. At least he wouldn't miss the magic of his house totally, even if he wasn't here to see it for himself.

Just as she was about to turn the laptop off she heard a ping, announcing the arrival of an e-mail. Thinking it might be from Ginny, informing her of the latest in a long line of pregnancy-related stories about absent-mindedness, she almost ignored it, but at the last minute she clicked on the little window and opened up the message.

She blinked and opened her eyes a little wider. It was from Mark. He must be online right now.

Hi Ellie
Thanks for the update on the plumbing situation. I'm sure you'll be glad to have your own space when the repairs are finished in your apartment. Feel free to decorate as you'd like.
I'm glad the wisteria is stunning and the roses are happy!!! I didn't realise you were a poet as well as a housekeeper ;-)
Mark.

What a cheek! Still, she couldn't erase the image of Mark's devil-may-care smile as she read it, and she was smiling too when she typed back her reply.

Fine. Now I know my boss is a Philistine I won't bother sending any similar observations with my next message!

Of course he couldn't leave it at that. And a rapid e-mail battle ensued. Ellie was laughing out loud when she finally admitted defeat and switched the laptop off. Maybe he was busy, after all. Maybe this whole 'deal' thing wasn't just an excuse to avoid her.

And that was how communication continued the next week or so. The e-mails got less businesslike and more chatty. Mark always added winky faces made out of colons and semi-colons—Sam would have said that he used far too many exclamation marks—and Ellie forgot her threat not to tell him anything about Larkford and ended up describing the way the wonderful house looked in the pale dawn light, losing herself in the images and getting all flowery about it…

And Mark, true to form, would reply with a teasing quip and burst her lyrical little bubble, causing her to laugh out loud and send back something equally pithy. She decided it was nice to communicate with someone who didn't remind her constantly of what she'd been like before the accident, who just accepted her for who she was now and didn't patronise her. He wasn't just her boss now; he was an ally.

But she knew he couldn't be any more than that. And that was fine, because that was exactly how she wanted it. Really, it was.

* * *

London late at night was stunning. Mark pressed his forehead against the plate-glass wall that filled one side of his living room and used his own shadow to block out the reflection of his flat so he could see the city beyond. Multi-coloured lights blinked on the black river below, endlessly dancing but never wearying.

When he'd bought this place he hadn't thought he'd get tired of this view, but lately he'd found himself wanting to trade it in for something else. Maybe a leafy square in Fitzrovia or a renovated warehouse near the docks?

He decided to distract himself from his restlessness by turning on the TV, but everything seemed pointless, so he wandered into his bedroom, crashed so hard onto the bed that it murmured in complaint, then picked up the book on his bedside table. *A Beginner's Guide to Head Injuries.* Only one more chapter to go and he'd be finished.

He got it now. Why Ellie had moments where she zoned out, why she forgot common words. It wasn't just that she was scatterbrained. Not that it mattered, anyway. And he wasn't entirely sure that *all* of Ellie's unique qualities were down to a rather nasty bump on the head. He had the feeling that even if the head injury could be factored out of the equation she'd still be pretty unique.

He read to the end of the bibliography and put the book back where he'd got it from. He hadn't checked his e-mail yet this evening, had he? And he had started to look forward to Ellie's slightly off-on-a-tangent e-mails. She had a way of making him feel as if he were right there at Larkford, with her little stories about village life and descriptions of which plants were in flower in the garden.

Bluebells.

In her last e-mail she'd said that she'd seen a carpet of bluebells in the woodland at the fringes of the estate. Although he'd never been a man to watch gardening programmes, or take long country walks to 'absorb nature', he'd suddenly wanted to stand in the shade of an old oak tree and see the blue haze of flowers for himself. He wanted to see Ellie smile and turn to him, as if she were sharing a secret with him…

No.

He couldn't think that way. He liked Ellie. He respected her. Hell, he was even attracted to her—majorly—but he couldn't go down that path.

It had been a long time since he'd held a woman in such high regard. And that was why this was dangerous. All the things he thought about Ellie… Well, they were the basis for a good relationship. Friendship, compatibility, chemistry. But he couldn't risk it. And not just for himself. What about Ellie? He wasn't the man for her. She didn't need someone who would probably cause her even more pain.

He jumped off the bed and started moving. Not that he had any particular destination in mind. He just seemed to get a burst of speed whenever he thought about a certain housekeeper.

And that was why he'd stayed away from Larkford. Because he was scared of what he was starting to feel for her. Yet even then she'd burrowed even further under his skin. Staying away hadn't worked, had it?

He found himself by the window in the living room again, and placed his palm on the glass.

So why was he here? Bored and wishing he was somewhere else? If keeping his distance hadn't worked, he might as well go and enjoy the house he'd bought for himself, because that was what he really wanted to do.

He wanted to go and see the bluebells for himself.

The gentle chiming of distant church bells roused Ellie from her Saturday morning slumber. Almost subconsciously she counted the chimes, not realising when she'd started but knowing the total by the time they'd finished. Eight.

Warm sunlight filtered through the curtains. She half sat in bed and rubbed her eyes. Her mouth gaped in an unexpected yawn. She shuffled herself out of bed, threw back the curtains and drank in the beautiful morning. The plumbing in her apartment above the old stables was now all fixed and she'd moved in. While her little kitchen looked over the cobbled courtyard, her bedroom had a wonderful view over the gardens. They were glorious this morning, bursting with life. She felt decidedly lazy as she watched a bee worrying the clematis beneath her window. It seemed completely unimpressed with her and disappeared into the centre of a large purple flower.

She turned from the window, full of great ideas for an al fresco lunch, and the sun glinted off the picture frame on the windowsill. She stopped to look at it, head tipped on one side. The photo had been taken at Chloe's fourth birthday party. Chloe was grinning like the proverbial Cheshire cat, her freshly lit birthday cake in front of her on the table. Sam and Ellie leaned in behind her, faces warmed by the glow of the candles.

They all looked so happy. She kissed her index finger and pressed it onto the glass where Chloe's smile was. It had been a wonderful day.

The memory came easily and painlessly now. She smiled as she recalled the incessant squealing of little girls and the pungent smell of blown-out birthday candles. Chloe had spent the whole party bouncing up and down in excitement, even when she was devouring pink birthday cake. She remembered Sam's smile later that evening, when he'd silently beckoned her to come and look at Chloe. They'd crept through the post-party devastation into the lounge and found her fast asleep on the sofa, chocolate smeared all over her face and clutching the doll they had given her in her sticky hands.

She'd found it so hard to look at this photo in the past. Even so, she'd kept it on prominent display as a kind of punishment. What she was guilty of, she wasn't sure.

Being here when they weren't. Being alive.

Since their deaths she had lived life as if she was walking backwards—too terrified of the unfamiliar territory ahead to turn and face the future. She'd blindly shuffled through each day, just trying to keep going without meeting disaster again. Pain was to be avoided at all costs. No risk.

No attachments. But no love, either. Her smile dissolved completely.

What would Sam think of the way she'd been coping?

She knew exactly what he would say. Her face creased into a frown. She could almost see his hazel eyes scowling at her, the trademark tuft of wayward hair slipping over his forehead.

Life should never feel small, Ellie.

That was what he'd always told her. Despite her secure family background she'd always been a shy child, but Sam had seen beyond the reserve. He'd asked her to play tag while the other schoolchildren had ignored the quiet girl on the wooden bench with her coat pulled round her. She'd been desperate to join in, but much too scared to get up and ask in case they laughed and ran away. But Sam had won her over with his gentle smile as he'd grabbed her hand and pulled her off the bench. Within minutes she'd been running after him, the wind in her hair and a smile beneath her rosy cheeks.

It had always been like that with Sam. He had encouraged her to dare, to believe. To make life count.

'Sorry, sweetheart,' she whispered, the glass misting as she talked to his face in the photo.

She sighed and pulled her tatty robe from its hook on the back of the door. Since the incident in Mark's car, she'd felt different. Liberated, somehow. Perhaps the whole embarrassing scenario had done some good after all. She'd been clutching on to her grief for so long, and her reaction to Mark's driving had finally provided an outlet—the last great emotional lurch in her rollercoaster stay at Larkford so far.

Ever since she had got here she'd been plunging into some forgotten feeling—panic, shame, anger—desire, even. She'd experienced them all in vivid richness. And somehow Mark Wilder stood in the middle of the maelstrom. Instead of making her feel safe, as Sam had, he made her feel nervous, excited and confused all at once. It was as if the universe had shifted a little when she wasn't looking and she suddenly found herself off-balance when he was around.

Yet he'd surprised her with his understanding and sensitivity. Not once had she felt judged for her behaviour that afternoon. It had been so nice to sink into his strong arms and know that she wasn't alone.

She tied the sash of her gown in a lumpy knot. With a heavy sigh she acknowledged that her relationship with Mark had changed in that moment. A boundary had been crossed as she had stood shivering against him in the lane.

She'd also noticed a change in Mark in the couple of weeks since he'd started living at Larkford again. But the way he was treating her now made her feel uncomfortable in a completely new way. Now he came home more evenings than he stayed away, even though the hour's drive from London could double if the motorway traffic was bad. He was always witty and entertaining, and she no longer fumed at his humour, but laughed along with it. There was even the odd quip at her expense, but it was a gentle nudge rather than sarcastic teasing.

He obviously thought she was too fragile to be toyed with now. What a pity, because suddenly she was ready to find out if there was an upside to all these impulses and strong emotions she'd inherited from the accident, to see if love and joy and happiness might just be brighter and more multi-coloured than they had ever been before.

Ellie was working on a salad for lunch when she heard a car pulling up outside. That was odd. She'd assumed Mark had been sleeping late, because he'd had to attend a function the night before, but that sounded like his car. She blinked in surprise when he strode into the kitchen a few moments later.

'You're up early,' she said, inspecting a bottle of rice vinegar to see how much was left—a complete cover for the fact her insides were doing the tango. He still made her catch her breath every time he walked into the room, but it was different. It wasn't all about hormones fizzing and pure physical reactions. Somehow those sensations had grown beyond the superficial things they were, and now she sometimes felt as if there was a dull ache inside her chest that grew stronger the closer he was to her.

'I had things to do,' he said.

She noticed the little shopping bag he was carrying with the logo of a high-end electrical store and shook her head. '*More* gadgets?' He was a typical man in that respect.

Instead of giving her a boyish grin and proudly showing off his latest piece of kit, he just looked a little awkward as he nodded his answer to her question.

'Actually, I bought this for you.'

Ellie put the vinegar bottle down on the counter and stared at him. 'For me?'

Mark handed her the bag and she pulled a small glossy box from it. A handheld computer. She stared at it, hardly knowing what to say.

'You got me a PDA?'

He nodded again, still unusually serious and silent. 'You can link it up to the laptop and keep all your calendars and notes with you wherever you go. It even has a voice recorder function. I thought it might be…you know…useful when you need to make a note of something in a hurry, before you forget.'

Ellie felt like crying. She hadn't even thought of using something like this, but it was perfect. Just what she needed.

'Thank you,' she said, her voice wavering. 'Why did you…? I mean, what made you think of getting me this?'

He shuffled backwards. 'Just something I read…'

She frowned at him. Where was the normally cocky and devil-may-care Mark Wilder? Why was he looking so sheepish?

Oh, great. He'd been researching her condition—probably read up on it on the Internet. While it was still an incredibly sweet gesture, it just confirmed that his view of her had changed. Now she was just the poor brain-damaged housekeeper who couldn't keep her facts straight without the help of a bit of technology.

She wanted to be cross with him, but she couldn't rev up the energy. Instead she put the box back in the bag and stowed it in an empty cupboard. 'I'll have a look properly later.'

'You like it? You think it'll be useful?'

He looked so hopeful, so eager, that she couldn't help but smile and nod. 'It's wonderful. It'll be a big help.'

And it would. There was no need to be sad about a tiny computer just because it signalled what she knew already—that anything more than a professional relationship between them was a total impossibility.

Mark grinned. Suddenly he was back to his old self: cheeky, confident…impossible. Ellie picked up a cook's knife and went back to chopping something—anything—to keep her mind occupied and her pulse even. But after a few moments he walked over to the chopping board and looked over her shoulder. Ellie fanned her face. It was very warm. Had he closed the window? She glanced over at the French doors, but the embroidered muslin panels were still billowing gently.

'What are you cooking?'

Ellie put the knife down a little too quickly. It clattered on the worktop. Despite the fact her brain told her the crush she had on Mark was pointless, the neural pathways carrying that information to her body seemed to have gone on strike.

'Vietnamese salad,' she said, the words tumbling out.

'Which is—?' He waved his hand in a circular motion as her mouth moved soundlessly.

'Chicken and noodles and a few vegetables, with a sweet chilli dressing,' she replied, a wobbly finger pointing to each of the ingredients in turn.

Great! Now she was babbling like a bad TV chef.

His cheek twitched, yet his face remained a mask of cool composure. 'Hot stuff, then?'

Under different circumstances, Ellie would have thought he was flirting with her. Heat licked at the soles of her feet. She swallowed. 'It depends on the size of the chilli.'

The look her gave her was positively wicked. 'And you girls try and tell us boys that size doesn't matter.'

Ellie almost choked.

Mark picked up the half-chopped chilli from the chopping board. 'How hot is this one?'

Ellie tried very hard to focus on the bright red chilli and not on Mark's warm brown eyes.

'Medium, sort of. The small ones are the hottest, funnily enough.'

Stop babbling! He already knows that. Everybody knows that!

She bit her lip and turned to peel the outer stem off a stick of lemongrass.

'Do you want this back?'

She felt Mark's breath warm on the back of her neck as he stood close behind her. She failed to still the tiny shiver that rippled up her spine as she turned slightly to take the chilli back from him.

'Thank you.'

She carefully eased it from his grasp, avoiding brushing his fingers, and offered up a silent *hallelujah* as Mark stepped back and headed for the door.

'I'm going for a shower.'

'Okay. Let me know if you want any of this when you come out.'

He ran his hand through his hair and rubbed the corner of one eye with his thumb. That early-morning start must be catching up with him.

But then she realised what he was about to do. 'Don't put your—'

Mark yelped, screwed his eyes shut tight and slapped his hands to his face. She rushed over to him, wincing in sympathy. She peeled the hand from his face and led him over to one of the break-fast stools, where she ordered him to sit down. His right eye was squeezed shut and watering.

'Try and open your eyes,' she said gently.

'Very funny!'

'I mean it. If you can manage to open them and blink a bit, the eye can do its job and wash the chilli juice away. It works a lot faster than sitting there with your fingers pressing into your eyeballs, making it worse!'

Mark groaned again, removed his hand and attempted to prise his watery eyelids apart.

'Wait there!' she ordered, dashing to the sink and washing her hands vigorously with washing-up liquid and scrubbing under her nails with a little brush.

'Here, let me see.'

She moved in close and delicately placed a thumb on the smooth skin near Mark's eye. He flinched.

'Sorry! Did I hurt you?'

'Um…no, it's okay.'

She gently pulled downwards, helping to open his eye. 'It looks a bit pink. Is it still stinging? Try blinking a few more times.'

'It's fading now, thank you, Nurse. How did you know what to do?'

She blushed. 'You think with a memory like mine that I haven't done this to myself a million times?'

Mark's laugh was deep and throaty. He blinked a few more times, opened his good eye, then attempted to do the same with the other, but it stayed stubbornly at half-mast.

Ellie's partial smile evaporated as she became conscious of the warmth radiating from him. They were practically nose to nose. He was sitting on the stool, one long leg braced against the floor, the other hooked on the bottom rung. She was standing between his legs, only inches from his chest. She knew she should move. Mark was looking back at her through bleary eyes. She picked a spot on the floor between her feet and stared at it.

'You're lucky,' she said, succeeding in inching backwards slightly.

Try not to look at him.

'You only touched the chilli briefly. It would have been much worse if you'd been chopping them...'

Mark caught her hand as she attempted to shuffle back further. She made the mistake of looking up. A soft, tender look was in his eyes, despite the fact that one eyeball was still pink and watery.

'Thank you, Ellie.' The sincerity in his tone was making her feel all quivery.

She managed to shift her gaze to her hand, still covered by his. Static electricity lifted the hairs on her arm.

'That's—that's all right,' she stammered. Her hand jerked from his as she shook herself loose. She turned and headed for the door. 'I'll go and have that shower now, then,' she added.

Perhaps a cold one.

She started to scuttle off down the passageway.

'Ellie…?' he called after her, a laugh underscoring his words.

The urge to keep going was powerful, but she turned and popped her head back through the open door. 'Yes?'

Mark was grinning at her. She had the sudden sinking feeling she didn't want to know why.

'*I* was going to have a shower, remember? *You* were cooking.'

Ellie closed her eyes gently and darted a moist tongue over her bottom lip, trying to work out how to salvage the situation. She looked at Mark with her best matter-of-fact expression. 'Of course.'

For some reason he looked very pleased with himself. He wasn't going to tease her about this for months to come, was he? What if he guessed it was him who had got her all in a fluster?

Once her cotton wool legs had taken her back to the chopping board she set about peeling the garlic, trying to block Mark's view of her shaking hands with her body. She heard the scrape of his stool across the floor as he rose from his seat. Every part of her body strained to hear his movements as he left the room. She stripped the skin off a clove of garlic, leaving it vulnerable and naked, and listened to Mark whistling something chirpy as he bounded up the stairs at least two at a time.

CHAPTER EIGHT

'MARK!'

His head snapped up. Nicole, his PA, stood with hands on hips, a buff folder clutched in one hand, scowling hard. This wasn't good news.

'Huh?'

'What is wrong with you this morning? That has to be the fifth time I've caught you admiring the London skyline while ignoring every word I say. You're making me feel like my old maths teacher, Mrs McGill.'

Mark stopped staring through the glass wall of his office and turned to face Nicole fully. She was right. He hadn't been paying attention. But now that he was she still wasn't making any sense.

'What?'

'She was always throwing chalk at Billy Thomas for staring out the window during double algebra. I mean it, Mark! If you make me sound like Mrs McGill I'm going to do something drastic.'

He hunched over his desk and scribbled feverishly away on the pad in front of him. Nicole flopped into the chair on the other side of the desk and massaged her temple with her free hand.

'What are you doing now? I'm feeling too grotty for your stupid games.'

When he had scrawled a handful of lines, he ripped the sheet off and thrust it in Nicole's direction. She snatched it from his hand and started to read it out loud.

'"I will not daydream in Mrs McGill's class. I will not daydream in—" Very funny!'

He easily dodged her missile as she crumpled the paper into a ball and threw it back at him. He did the puppy-dog thing with his eyes he knew she could never resist.

'Sorry, Miss.'

'You'd better be! You were saying something about pushing the record company for a three-sixty-degree contract for the new band's next deal, and then you just drifted off.'

'Sorry, Nic. I promise I'm listening now.'

He rested his elbows on the desk and propped his chin on his fists, deliberately focusing on her and only her.

'And I need to know what you want to do about

this video shoot. We've only got five days before we leave for the Caribbean, and Kat's in a state because Razor went AWOL. The director has changed his mind about one of the locations, and the stylist has had a strop and isn't taking any of my calls.'

Mark did his best to listen as Nicole continued to brief him on the latest string of disasters to hit the upcoming shoot. It had been a nightmare from start to finish. He was starting to wish they'd opted for the other treatment, which had involved lots of time on a soggy moor in Scotland. When they'd set it up he'd been looking forward to going to Antigua. He'd planned on taking a few days off after the shoot—the closest thing to a holiday he was going to get this year.

But now the date was looming close he was starting to wish he could wriggle out of it. He didn't want to leave Larkford. A week on the other side of the planet would be a week away from Ellie. Coming into London was different. He was away for the day, but in the evening he would be stranded on the M25 in the rush-hour traffic with a smile on his face, knowing he was on the way home.

Home. Ellie had made his house a home. He loved arriving back there and seeing a warm glow in the windows instead of faceless black. He would park his car, walk through the door and find Ellie pottering in the kitchen, cooking up something fabulous.

He had started to fantasise that she was there waiting for him, not because he paid her to, but because she wanted to be.

She worked so hard. Now he'd read up on brain injuries he understood how difficult it must be for her. And she never seemed to want a day off to go home. Perhaps there were too many memories waiting for her there. But it would be good if he could get her to relax now she had the household running like clockwork. He'd even cover the cost of a holiday if he thought she'd accept it from him. He almost felt guilty for jetting off to the Caribbean and leaving her behind.

Maybe there was something he could do about that…

Nicole slapped her folder down so hard that the papers on Mark's desk lifted in the resultant breeze.

'If you're not going to listen, I'm going for a girlie chat with Emma at the end of the hall!'

He was only partially aware of the slam of the door and the meant-to-be-heard muttering as she click-clacked out of the office and down the hallway. He swung his chair round again and continued studying the busy city below. The Thames glinted between the mixture of glass office blocks and the pollution-stained masonry of older buildings.

The last few weeks had been both heaven and hell.

The prickly, reclusive Ellie who had arrived at Larkford in the spring was only a memory. The Ellie he returned to each night was warm and caring and funny. Clever and resourceful. He loved hanging around the kitchen watching her cook, savouring each bite of the meal and making it last as long as possible to prolong his time in her company. He always felt a little deflated when the coffee cups were cleared away and the mechanical whooshing of the dishwasher was the only sound in the kitchen.

She was still a little shy, but it added to her charm. He loved the way she was totally original— one of a kind.

Mark stood up. The afternoon sun was bouncing off the windows of the other office blocks, giving the whole city a warm yellow glow. He took a moment to process the revelation that had just hit him smack between the eyes.

He loved her.

His stomach lurched as he recognised his own vulnerability. Whether she knew it or not, that fragile woman had tremendous power over him.

But he didn't want to push her, even if he guessed she might be feeling at least some of what he was feeling. He watched a jet puff out its white trail in the clear blue sky, the plane so high up it was only a silver speck in the air. Part of him exulted at the knowledge that she found him attractive, that he put her off-balance, but another part of him ached with the uncertainty of any deeper feelings on her part.

'I need a sign!' he whispered, waiting for something to happen.

But the plane kept on its course, its trail a no-nonsense line. No writing appeared in the sky saying *Go for it*. He scanned the horizon for a hint of divine thunderbolts, but the pale clouds refused to comment.

He continued to ponder his position as he sat behind a truck on the M25 later that evening. The crawling traffic gave him plenty of time for self-analysis. He sat for many minutes trying to predict the outcome of any romantic entanglement with Ellie and decided that prophecy was not his thing. It didn't matter, anyway. Whether she loved him back or not wouldn't change how he felt about her. He would just have to be patient. Wait in this horrible limbo until a sign appeared.

Butterflies wrestled in his belly as he turned the

car into his driveway. His pulse quickened as he jumped from the car and bounded up the steps to the front door. As he put the key in the lock a mouthwatering aroma assaulted his nostrils. He followed the trail into the kitchen. Ellie bobbed up from behind the kitchen counter, causing his already racing heart to skip a beat.

'That was good timing! I was just about to dish up. You're much later than you said.'

'Traffic jam,' he said absently, his eyes following her every move. She reached to get a couple of plates from the cupboard and passed them to him.

'Your PA called about an hour ago.'

Ah. He'd forgotten all about Nic, and had left the office without telling her.

'She said she will not be coming back into work until you ring and tell her she is no longer Mrs McGill—whatever that means!' said Ellie, searching for the oven gloves and finding them in the dishwasher.

Mark reckoned an apologetic lunch somewhere nice would probably help. And maybe a big bunch of flowers. Nicole's bark was worse than her bite, and he didn't know what he would do without her. His stomach complained noisily, returning him to the present.

'What's for dinner?'

Ellie opened the oven door and stood back from the blast of hot air before she reached inside to remove a scalding-hot earthenware dish. She looked very pink as she stood straight. If it wasn't for the heat from the oven, he could have sworn she was blushing.

'Shepherd's Pie.'

Mark almost dropped the plates he was holding.

'Thank you,' he mouthed to the ceiling, before following her to the table.

Ellie was in the chemist's in the village, picking up some supplies, when her mobile rang. The caller ID told her it was Mark, and she took a steadying breath before she punched the button to answer.

'Hello?'

'It's me. Are you busy?'

Ellie looked at the tube of toothpaste, a box of plasters and the hand soap in her shopping basket. 'I'm in the village shopping, but I'll be finished in a few minutes. Do you want me to come straight back?'

'Yes. I've got a bit of an emergency on my hands.'

And, without explaining anything further, he rang off. Ellie stared at the phone. Very mysterious. She quickly paid for the items in her basket and hurried back along the lane to Larkford Place, cutting through the gardens to make her journey quicker.

When she reached the back door and entered the kitchen she found it all quiet. Guessing Mark must be in his study, she dumped her shopping bag on the counter, prised off her trainers and socks—it was too hot for shoes—and headed off to find him.

He was sitting behind his desk listening to someone on the other end of the phone when she poked her head round the half-open door. She coughed gently and he motioned for her to come in and sit down, still listening to whoever it was on the line.

She sat in the small but rather comfortable leather chair on the opposite side of the desk and waited, noticing as she did so that the colour of her painted toenails clashed with the rug. He finished the call without saying much but 'mmm-hmm' and 'bye', and replaced the phone carefully in its cradle before looking at her.

'I have an idea to run past you. I hope you don't mind?'

Ellie shook her head. Although she was a bit puzzled as to why Mark would want her help with what was obviously a business problem.

'I'm due to fly to Antigua at the end of the week and my PA, vital to keeping me organised during what is likely to be a chaotic few days, has come down with the flu. I need someone to fill in for her.'

Ellie studied her toenails again. Tangerine really didn't go with the aubergine shapes on the abstract rug.

'Can't someone from the office fill in?'

'Difficult. The whole place is in turmoil with a newly signed band. Their first single is out this week and it's all hands on deck. Anyone who isn't already with a client is involved in that. I did have two people in mind, but one is on holiday and the other is pregnant and throwing up every ten minutes. I seem to have run out of employees to commandeer.'

Ellie smiled at that. Nobody to boss around? What a hardship.

When she looked up, a wolfish grin was on his lips.

'Well, *almost* run out of employees…' he added.

She didn't like the look of that smile. She felt like Little Red Riding Hood, lost in the woods. Mark's eyeballs didn't move a millimetre as he stared straight at her. Ellie began to shake her head.

No way! Don't you even think it!

He nodded in slow motion as her ringlets

bounced from side to side. Without warning he sprang from his side of the desk and bounded towards her. He crouched in front of her and tugged her hands into his.

'I have got one employee who could help me out.'

Her heartbeat accelerated. It was difficult to think whilst looking into those bottomless brown eyes.

'Come on, Ellie. I know you can do this. Charlie told me about how you used to be a PA.'

Ellie tried to stammer *no,* but her mouth refused to co-operate. His eyes looked like a spaniel's. She'd bet this was the puppy-dog thing Charlie had warned her about. It would be like stamping on a poor abandoned animal if she refused. And it would be to help Mark out of a tight spot. She couldn't really do this, could she?

Mark pressed on while he had the advantage.

'Look at the way you run the house. You're quick to pick things up, and you've got bags of initiative. Even with all your challenges you seem to handle any unexpected thing I throw at you. I know this is a different ball game, but I have confidence in you. Please!'

Ellie grabbed the lifeline he had thrown at her. 'The house!' she blurted out.

Mark frowned. 'What house?'

'This one! We can't leave it unattended. Who's going to look after it?' She let out a relieved sigh and relaxed into the padded leather chair, feeling oddly deflated at her own success.

'Mrs Timms could manage for a few days. I've asked her already and she said her daughter would be able to help her out.'

Ellie sat, mouth open, trying to find another valid objection. She'd only just got used to Larkford. To go somewhere else, somewhere completely foreign—literally—and do work she wasn't used to doing. Well, the idea was just plain terrifying. And she hadn't even factored in how difficult it would be to spend days upon end in a tropical paradise working even more closely with Mark.

He was smiling at her, his voice low and rich. Ellie could feel herself slipping. 'Mrs Timms used to work here before you started. Mind you, she wasn't nearly as good—or pretty.' His eyes twinkled. 'And she smelled of peppermints and disinfectant—'

'Mark!'

'I know. Not important.'

He took hold of her hands again, eyes pleading. 'It's only for a few days. I just need someone to handle the red tape while I look after fragile egos and deal with hissy fits—and that's just the tea lady I'm talking about.'

Ellie couldn't help laughing. She suspected he could persuade her that black was white if he put his mind to it.

She folded her arms across her chest. 'I will *think* about it.'

'Basket case!'

Ellie mumbled to herself as she watched the planes taxiing back and forth in the evening haze, her nose pressed hard against the plate-glass wall of Heathrow's first class lounge. The sunset was tarnished by the pollution of the busy airport.

What an idiot to think she could do this.

She turned, leaning back on the cold window to survey her fellow travellers sprawled over the comfy sofas on the far side of the lounge. Mark was chatting to Kat and the other members of her entourage. He looked completely at ease. In fact he'd been looking pretty darn pleased with himself since she'd told him she would fill in for his sick PA at breakfast this morning.

Ellie sighed and banged the back of her head lightly against the glass. She'd made a valiant attempt to say no to Mark's offer, but she hadn't quite been able to bring herself to turn him down.

Of course her decision had everything to do with a free trip to Antigua, and nothing at all to do with spending the next few days with Mark instead of rattling round Larkford Place on her own. At least that was what she'd thought this morning. Somehow the universe had done a one-eighty between then and now. The fantasy of jetting off to a palm tree filled island in a sarong and flip-flops had fallen flat once they had arrived at the airport. Well, slightly before that, Ellie admitted, looking down at her un-flip-flopped feet and sarong-less legs.

She hadn't realised they were going to be travelling with Kat and her 'people'. Immediately she'd gone into tortoise mode, feeling she had nothing much in common with the assorted bunch of strangers. Kat seemed nice—very young, and much shorter than she'd expected.

She studied the other members of the entourage. There was a tall, burly guy with a pair of shades who she presumed was a bodyguard or something. The girl with the funky white-blonde hair had to be a make-up artist or hairdresser. But she couldn't even guess what the others did. The woman in the lurid boob tube could be Kat's personal grape-peeler for all she knew.

The young guy with the pierced nose finished telling a funny story and the whole group erupted into laughter. Ellie's eyes followed Mark's every move as he grinned away, pleased with the reaction. The funky-haired woman put a pressureless hand on his arm as she wiped a tear from her eye.

Ellie frowned and turned back to face the anonymous jets parading round the runway. Her forehead met the cool glass with a delicate thud.

Basket case.

At thirty-five-thousand feet she was still wondering what she was doing with these people. Sure, she'd been on aeroplanes before, but it had been rubber food, cramped leg room and fighting about who had the armrest. Not this. Not champagne and seats you could fit a small family into. It all seemed so foreign—yet it shouldn't. Nobody else seemed to be pining for garish seat covers and lager louts singing football songs.

She felt like an impostor. Any minute now people would start pointing and staring, and she'd be dragged back to Economy, where she belonged. This wasn't her world. What a huge mistake to think she could slide in here with Mark and find it a perfect fit.

However, the outsize chair was definitely comfy, and she sank into it, her eyelids closing of their own accord.

The next thing she was aware of was something brushing her cheek, something soft and slightly moist. She swatted it away without opening her eyes.

'Ow!'

She pulled her eyelids apart with enough force to unstick her eyelashes and squinted at the fuzzy shape in front of her. As it came into focus she realised it was Mark, and his lips were slightly pursed.

'Why are you holding your nose like that?' she asked, shifting in her seat to get a better look.

'I was trying to wake you up when you walloped me.'

'I didn't wallop. I swatted. There's a difference.' She rubbed the spot on her cheek that was still tickling her. 'And how did I end up hitting you on the nose? What were you doing that close?'

In the semi-dark of the cabin she could have sworn his face turned a shade pinker.

'I was just… Never mind what I was doing! I was waking you up because the pilot just announced we'd be landing in half an hour. I thought you'd want to get yourself together.'

She stretched her arms past her head, yawned and looked out of the window. It was so dark out there they could have been flying through a black hole.

'What time is it?'

'Our time or local time?'

'Whichever.'

'Well, it's just after midnight local time. At least we get a few extra hours to catch up on sleep.'

Ellie made a face. 'I think I could do with a whole week!'

He smiled, and she forgot to be grumpy.

'You know, you look very cute when you've just woken up,' he said.

Ellie snorted, then pulled a mirror out of her bag and inspected the damage. Just as she'd thought. All her mascara had migrated into a gloopy lump in one corner of her eye. Very cute.

'You need glasses, then,' she said as she threw the mirror onto her lap and searched for a tissue in a bag pocket.

'Here—let me.'

Before she could refuse he'd whipped a handkerchief out of his pocket with a flourish and tipped her chin towards him with his other hand.

He leaned so close all the hairs behind her ears stood on end. She did her absolute best not to look too pathetic as he gently dabbed her eye. Somehow, with him taking care of her like this, she didn't feel so lost.

That incident set the tone for the rest of the journey. When she hauled her cases off the carousel at baggage reclaim Mark was there with a trolley before she even blinked. He shepherded her into one of the cars that appeared like magic out at the front of the terminal and saw her settled at the hotel.

It had been so long since she'd felt like this. Safe. Taken care of. Not struggling to do everything by herself. It was very tempting to give in and forget they'd be home in a few days. And that, technically, she was being paid to look after him.

Ellie shivered as yet another spider scuttled across her foot. The first time one had crawled over her today she'd almost freaked out. Big time. But the cameras were rolling, filming at the first location for Kat's video, and she hadn't wanted to sprint round the set like a lunatic in front of the crew.

Or re-live the incident when they watched the rushes at the end of the day.

Or feature in some TV out-takes compilation next Christmas.

So, although she felt as if she'd imploded with the effort, she stifled the screams, put on a stoic face and stood her ground.

She sighed and ran her fingers through the damp curls sticking to her forehead. The whole crew was packed into a tight knot at the end of an idyllic bay where the narrow beach met the rocks. Ellie was hiding out in the jungle-like greenery that fringed the white-hot sand. Hence the spiders. She'd thought she'd do anything to escape something with eight legs, but the need for shade and even a few degrees less heat had overruled her natural instincts. It was only *after* they'd arrived at the hotel that Mark had explained that summer could be hot and horribly humid on the island. Most of the tourists came in the winter months.

Kat was knee-deep in water, singing along to the track that was due to be her next single. The surf behind her looked mighty inviting. Ellie was fantasising about diving into the sea, acting like a fish and hoping nobody would notice. Nice dream, but in reality she was stuck under the nearest palm tree, wilting, while everybody else did something vastly important.

The heat was making her clothes stick to her skin. Even her skin was sticking to her skin. She longed for the air-conditioned haven of the hotel. Typical of many resorts on the island, the elegant low-rise main building was surrounded by lush tropical gardens and luxurious cabins. She wanted to be doing jobs she knew how to do: faxing things, shredding things. An evil glint flickered in her eyes. She wanted to be stapling things—preferably to Mark's head.

No, that wasn't fair. It was her own fault she hadn't found out what she was letting herself in for. It was the jet lag making her tetchy. And she'd never been on friendly terms with this kind of heat. It made her hair frizz.

The director stood up and bellowed, 'Cut!'

The music died instantly, but Ellie knew the song so well by now that it kept playing inside her skull, pounding against her temples.

The director barked instructions to anyone within earshot.

'Baz, zoom out a little so I can see the sand. Jerry, check that last take to see if the light is still okay. Kat, my darling, could you just move to that rock on your left?' Kat waded obligingly to the rock and took up her position. 'That's it. Can you put one foot on top of it? Good.'

Ellie admired her stamina. They'd all been standing on this beach for most of the day. She'd have dived in and floated away hours ago if it she'd been in Kat's shoes. She massaged her forehead and listened to the pounding of the surf. She'd expected a little time to collect herself after they'd arrived, but it had been straight to work. No lounging by the pool under a yellow umbrella. No sipping coconut-flavoured cocktails in a hammock. Time really was money when video cameras were involved, it seemed.

'Playback!'

The director's yell was like a crack from a shotgun. Birds scattered from the treetops in terror. Ellie checked her clipboard. All her tasks were done. There was nothing left to do but drift over towards the director and watch Kat's progress on one of the boxy little monitors.

The minute hand on her watch dragged itself listlessly through the next few hours and the sun began to set. They moved position a few times, and each move meant ages of checking the lighting, setting up cameras and other kit. Then Kat would have to sing her song another thousand times, this time in close-up, this time on a long-shot. See? She was even starting to learn the lingo.

Just as the sun had finally set, and Ellie was about to scream with the monotony of it all, Mark suddenly waded into the sea and scooped Kat into his arms.

'Cut!' the director bellowed, impotent with fury.

Ellie could only imagine the myriad expletives scalding the tip of his tongue. He spluttered, searching for the right word to unlock the torrent. Ellie turned quickly to face the trees and hid a smile. The prima donna on this set was definitely not the singer!

Mark said nothing as he carried Kat out of the water, but his eyes were blazing a warning as clear as if he'd shouted it. The director swallowed his rant. Mark unhooked his arm from under Kat's knees and let her bare feet touch the ground in one controlled motion.

'That's a wrap for today, everybody,' he said.

His voice was calm, but everyone from the director to the runners knew that negotiations were useless. The generator coughed to a halt. No one moved.

Ellie broke the tense silence with a scurry of movement. She tugged a fluffy towel out of the bag of provisions she'd hauled along with her and slung it over Kat's shoulders. All that time standing in the water! The poor girl must be prune-like on the bottom half and baked on the top half. She glanced at Mark, and flushed as she saw the flicker of approval in his eyes.

Kat whispered her thanks as they headed to the speed boats that had brought them on the short trip round the coast into the small crescent-shaped bay. It had been chosen because they were practically guaranteed an uninterrupted shoot, with no onlookers or journalists to deal with as it was inaccessible by road.

Mark and Kat headed for the smallest boat, followed closely by Rufus, Kat's bodyguard—or personal protection officer, as he preferred to be called. Ellie trailed along behind, still feeling like a spare part. The rest of the crew concentrated on unplugging and packing the expensive technical thingummy-jigs in foam-padded metal cases. They would follow on shortly, in the larger two boats.

They arrived back at the small marina in the neighbouring bay and made their way to the cluster of anonymous black people-carriers that were waiting for them in the car park. Mark pulled Ellie back to let Kat and Rufus walk ahead.

'I'm going to wait here for our illustrious director and give him a piece of my mind. If he plans to roast Kat alive in the midday sun tomorrow he's going to have to think again.'

'You act more like her big brother than her manager.'

Mark frowned a little. 'Babysitting the star is part of my job description. On the business side, I wouldn't be doing my job if Kat couldn't finish the shoot.' His matter-of-fact manner softened. 'But you're right. I do feel protective towards her. It's easy to forget she's only seventeen and all her friends are still at school.'

He shielded his eyes with a hand and looked up the walkway after Kat as she slid the back door of the people-carrier open and climbed inside. 'She's a great kid. If she can get through the next couple of years without self-destructing she'll have a long and successful career.' He looked Ellie straight in the eye. 'It would be such a waste if she burns out.'

The compassion in his eyes made something inside her feel very gooey indeed. She'd thought Work Mark would be different—harder, more remote. If it were possible, he was even nicer than Home Mark.

He turned away, stuffed his hands in his pockets and scoured the headland for a hint of the other boats.

'She's had a tough time recently,' he said, and

turned back towards her. 'Will you look after her for me while I wait here?'

Ellie rubbed his arm lightly and nodded.

The clouds in Mark's expression were banished by a smile. He planted a feather-soft kiss on the tip of her nose and walked down the pontoons to wait by the empty berths.

That kiss was the cherry on top of the weird feelings she'd been having since they'd arrived in Antigua less than twenty-four hours ago. It was as if she was in a parallel universe where, even though she was working for Mark, the 'employer' and 'employee' labels they'd stuck on themselves had peeled off in the heat, leaving only a man and a woman who were really, really attracted to each other.

CHAPTER NINE

WHEN Ellie reached the car she tapped on the mirrored window, assuming that Kat was taking advantage of the relative privacy to change her clothes.

'Ellie?'

'Yes. Are you okay?'

An exasperated grunt preceded Kat's reply. 'Well, yes and no—it's okay to open the door.'

Ellie eased the sliding door open an inch or two. Kat looked more like a half-drowned cat than a sex kitten. Her eyes pleaded and she wore a weary smile.

'The knot in my bikini top won't come undone.'

'Come here.' She turned Kat to face the other way with the same kind of deft handling that she had used when making Chloe stand still to have her hair brushed. As Ellie set to work on the knot she couldn't help noticing the angry pink on Kat's shoulders.

'You look like you've caught the sun, despite the lotion you slathered on.'

'Great. And I've got to do it all over again tomorrow.'

Ellie released the tangle in the bikini top straps and stood back outside the car as Kat finished changing, leaving the door slightly ajar so she could catch her conversation.

'The director will probably have me snorkelling with sharks or something,' Kat said with a tired laugh.

'I'm sure Mark would have something to say about that.'

'He's great, isn't he?'

Ellie tried not to comment for fear of incriminating herself. She made what she hoped was an ambiguous noise to cover all eventualities, but knew she'd failed when Kat slid the door open for Ellie to climb in. Kat had obviously absorbed some of Mark's mannerisms while she'd been working with him, because that smirk was pure Wilder. Ellie busied herself by doing up her seat belt.

Kat leaned across and whispered in a conspiratorial manner, 'Don't worry. Your secret is safe with me.'

Ellie's eyes jumped from Kat to the back of Rufus's head as he drove the car out of the car park.

'Don't worry about him, Ellie. Rufus knows all my secrets and his lips are sealed—aren't they, Rufus?'

Rufus agreed by remaining silent, his thick neck motionless.

'See?'

Ellie groaned. Was she really so transparent that every passing stranger could read the contents of her head?

'I trust Mark one hundred percent,' Kat said, giving her a meaningful look. 'Some managers sign up young talent and work them like crazy until they drop. Then it's on to the next fresh young thing. But Mark's not like that. He always looks after me.'

Kat looked down at her lap. 'I just split up from my boyfriend. I thought he was perfect. They do say love is blind, don't they?'

Ellie squeezed her hand softly. Kat sniffed.

'It's hard to get over it when I see pictures of him in the papers almost every day. On a beach with some girl. In a nightclub with some other girl. At a premiere with—you get the picture, right? But Mark has been great. I can't count the number of times he's handed me tissues as I told him the latest sob story.' A fat tear rolled down her cheek and she sighed and looked out of the window at the lush tropical scenery. 'Sometimes I wish I could run away for a bit and have a little time to myself to get over it. But just when I think I'm on my own, *bam*! There's a telephoto lens sticking out the bushes. I can see the headlines already: "Kat's Secret Anguish Over Split."'

Ellie felt her own eyes grow wet. Mark was right. Kat was a great girl, and she lived a difficult life for a seventeen-year-old. When she spoke, there was a croaky edge to her voice.

'My husband used give me a piece of advice that I'm going to pass on to you—'

Kat jumped round to face her, eyes stretching wide open.

'You're married!'

'I *was* married. I'm not now,' Ellie said quickly. 'Long story. Anyway, Sam used to tell me that life should never feel small. I'm a bit of a tortoise by nature, I'm afraid, much happier if I'm all tucked in inside my shell, where I'm safe and warm. But I'm starting to remember that *safe and warm* can be incredibly dull and lonely. Sometimes we've just got to have the courage to step out and live, no matter what happens.' She turned to look Kat in the eye. 'I can see that kind of strength in you. You *will* get through this.'

They hugged as far as the seat belts would allow, then Kat shifted in her seat and stared out the window.

'What happened to…to your…? Did you get a divorce?'

Ellie tried to eliminate any trace of emotion in her voice. 'No. He died.'

Kat's head snapped round. An involuntary hand covered her mouth, trying to catch the words that had already escaped.

'And here's me snivelling about a man who doesn't deserve my tears…'

Ellie's smile was braver than she felt. 'It's okay.'

'When did it…? I mean, how did he…?'

'He and my daughter were killed in a car accident a few years ago.' Ellie glanced down at the date function on her watch. 'In fact, it will be exactly four years in a week's time.'

A tear ran down Kat's face. 'Oh, Ellie!'

'Don't you start!' She pressed the heels of her hands into her own soggy eyes. 'Now you've got me going.'

A small noise from the front seat made them both look up. Did she really see Rufus dab a finger under his eye?

'Does Mark know?'

Ellie nodded. 'About my family? Yes.'

'No, I mean about next Friday.'

Ellie shook her head as the car pulled up under the canopied front awning of their hotel. Rufus got out of the car, leaving it to the valet, and headed round to open Kat's door for her.

Kat continued, despite Ellie's shaking head. 'You should tell him—you ought to, Ellie. He's really sweet and supportive. You know, he even postponed an important business trip to come to an awards thing a couple of months ago. I was petrified—more of winning than of sinking into the background—and Mark cancelled everything to be there for me. You could do with a friend like that right now.'

Ellie had no chance to respond as Rufus opened the door and bundled Kat through the hotel lobby before anyone could mob her. Ellie followed in their wake, taking advantage of the invisible path before it was filled by holidaymakers and bell-boys with trolleys. They walked out into the hotel gardens and Kat headed for her cool white cabin with its low tiled roof and wraparound veranda. Ellie stood alone on the terrace steps and watched their progress. Just before the mismatched pair disappeared behind a clump of bushes lining the path, Ellie saw Kat mouth a message to her: *Tell him!*

Tell him? Tell him *what*, exactly? There was so much to choose from.

Tell him it was the first time the dreaded anniversary hadn't filled her with panic? That something had made it different this year, and that he was the something? There was too much to say, and most of it needed to be left unsaid.

She weaved her way back through the bustling lobby, confident in the knowledge that no paparazzi were going to be somersaulting from the light fittings in order to snap *her* picture, thank goodness.

The yellow umbrellas by the pool were calling to her. Time to get intimately acquainted with an outlandish cocktail with pineapple bits and paper parasols. She marched up to the poolside bar and ordered one that came in a glass the size of a small goldfish bowl.

The thick icy liquid struggled its way up the straw and she aimlessly watched the tanned bodies diving into the pool.

Kat was right. Mark was sweet and loyal and dependable—absolutely nothing like her first impressions of him. She'd been so blinkered. But now… Now she could see it all.

It reminded her of the visual neglect she'd experienced for a couple of months following the accident. For a while she'd only been aware of half the things in her field of vision. The weird thing was she hadn't even realised anything was wrong. But she'd found reading confusing, because when she'd read a magazine she'd only seen half of each sentence on the page. And she'd only washed one side of her face. When the nurses had realised they'd developed strategies to help, and gradually, as her brain had started to heal itself, she'd been able to process information from both sides of her visual field again.

Why and how had she chosen to see only half of Mark? And only negative things too? Ellie put her glass down on the bar. She'd made up her mind about him, set its trajectory, before she'd even met him. Her thought patterns had got stuck in one of their grooves yet again.

But now she saw all of him…

Oh.

And she saw all of herself too—all the things she felt for him.

A jumble of images, sensations and smells hit her all at once. As if every moment she'd spent with Mark flashed before her eyes. All her blinkers dropped away and she felt as if she was floating, with nothing left to anchor her to cold, hard reality.

It was quite possible she was desperately in love with him. How could she not have known?

And how had this happened in the first place? He was nothing like Sam, and she'd always expected that happiness only came in that size and shape. How would it work with someone totally different? *Could* it work? Their lives were so different. Could she find joy in his fast-moving, flashbulb-popping world?

Talking to Kat earlier had stretched her conceptions of what being rich, successful and famous was like, had given her a fresh look at life from her side of the lens. Kat was surprisingly human. In fact she was just like thousands of other seventeen-year-olds who cried into their pillows every night because they'd fallen for the wrong guy.

Maybe it wasn't all as impossible as it seemed. Maybe she could have a future with Mark. Everybody needed love, whether they were rich or poor, somebody or nobody.

Her head swam. Too much pineapple-rum stuff on an empty stomach. This was no time to be thrashing this problem out.

What she needed was a clear head—and a shower.

And with that thought she plopped the straw back into the half-full cocktail glass and walked through the gardens to her cabin, thinking that even if she never qualified for the former she could definitely manage the latter.

A knock on the half-open slatted door of the cabin caused Ellie to jump off the sofa she'd been dozing on. For a second her mind was blank and she was totally in the present, hardly aware of where she was and what she'd been doing to make her so sleepy.

There was another knock, and she swivelled to face the veranda. She knew it was Mark standing out there, knew it in a way that had nothing to do with the height and shape of his silhouette and everything to do with the way her skin prickled in anticipation.

'Come in,' she called out, and then realised too late that she'd been fresh out of the shower when she'd collapsed on the sofa and was still dressed in her old pink robe. Too late to do anything about it now; he was already pushing the door fully open. She tried to smooth her damp hair down, and pulled at the edges of her robe to get rid of the gap.

'I…er…' He stopped and swallowed. Where was the carefree, free and easy Mark Wilder banter? Probably evaporated in the heat. He tried again. 'I wondered if…if you'd like to grab some dinner?'

'Oh. Okay. That would be lovely.'

Although they'd finished early, the third and final day of shooting had left her absolutely ravenous. On the previous couple of evenings they'd joined Kat and some of her entourage in the rather trendy hotel restaurant. Ellie had enjoyed the gourmet food, but had felt a bit superfluous to requirements.

'I'll just go and get dressed,' she said, pulling herself to her feet.

She wasn't really in the mood for sitting on the sidelines of another round of industry chat and gossip, but the only alternative was sitting alone in her room, and at least this way she got to be with Mark.

As she emerged from her bedroom, wearing a simple long skirt and spaghetti-strap top, she glanced at the clock. 'It's only four-thirty. Aren't we a bit early for dinner?'

'I've been up since six this morning and I'm starving,' Mark said. 'I don't know about you?'

Ellie nodded enthusiastically.

'Anyway, there's something I want you to see first.'

Instead of heading for the hotel restaurant, Mark set off in a different direction, his long legs helping him to stride ahead. She was too busy just keeping

up with him to ask questions. He led them into the
hotel car park, hopped into a Jeep with a driver at
the wheel and sat there, grinning at her, as if he'd
done the cleverest thing in the world.

Ellie put her hands on her hips. 'Where are we
going?'

She didn't add *alone together*.

'I'm taking you to the best place on the island.'

Ellie looked down at her floral-print skirt and
flip-flops. She wasn't really dressed for fine
dining. And she was too tired to be on her best behaviour. When she felt all fuzzy-headed like this
she knew she was apt to forget words and bump
into things more easily.

He patted the seat beside him and gave her a meaningful look. Ellie climbed in, too tired to be bothered
to walk back down to her cabin, flop onto her sofa
and dial Room Service. At least doing it Mark's way
she wasn't going to have to use her legs.

The driver put the Jeep into gear and they rattled
their way through the neatly manicured resort, but
it wasn't long before they'd left it behind them,
heading uphill. The road was lined with palms
and aloes and breadfruit trees. Occasionally she
saw pretty little clusters of yellow orchids dancing
in the light evening wind.

Ellie breathed out and relaxed back into her seat. This was lovely, actually. Although they'd been to three different locations over the island in the last three days, she'd always been too caught up with her clipboard and 'to do' lists, terrified of missing something, to sit back and admire the scenery. This island truly was stunning, everything a tropical paradise should be. The beaches were soft white sand, the sea shades of cobalt and turquoise. If it wasn't all so pretty it would be a giant cliché. But there was something comforting about having her expectations met rather than defied for once.

It was almost a shame that everything was over and they'd be flying back tomorrow. At least she assumed it was tomorrow. If Mark had told her the time of the flight, she'd already lost that bit of information in the maze of her brain.

Looking down the steep hill and out to sea, she asked, 'What time do we need to get to the airport tomorrow?'

Mark didn't answer right away, and eventually she stopped looking at the stupendous view and turned to face him.

'Mark?'

He looked away, studying the scenery through

the windscreen. 'Actually, I'd planned to take a break—stay on for a few more days.'

Oh.

That meant she'd be going home alone. Suddenly all the hours of flying she'd be doing seemed a lot emptier. She nodded, following Mark's lead and looking straight ahead.

Mark cleared his throat. 'And I wondered if maybe you wanted to stay on too? Have a holiday?'

Ellie found her voice was hoarse when it finally obliged and came out of her mouth. 'With you? On our own?'

'Yes.'

There was a long pause, and all the air that had been whipping past their faces, ruffling their hair, went still.

'I'm not ready to go home yet,' he added.

She glanced across at him, and her heart began to thud so hard she felt a little breathless. He didn't look like the normal, cocky Mark Wilder she knew at all. He looked serious and honest and just a little lost.

She had to look away. Scared that she might be imagining all the things she could see in his eyes. Scared this was just another impulse or trick her brain was playing on her.

'Neither am I,' she said softly.

And then the air began to move around them again. They both breathed out at the same time. After a few moments something tickled Ellie's hand. She didn't look, not wanting to spoil anything. And as Mark's fingers wound themselves round hers she felt something hard inside her melt.

The Jeep climbed higher and higher, the road twisting and turning, and the lush banana trees and palms gave way to scrub and cacti. Now she could see down into the harbour, dotted with the white triangles of hundreds of yachts, and somewhere in the distance she could hear the unmistakable sound of a steel band.

Moments later the Jeep swung round a corner and was parked not far from a few old military buildings, obviously left over from the days of British rule. Reluctantly she let Mark's hand slide from hers as he jumped out of the Jeep and then came round to her side to help her out. They left the Jeep behind and walked towards a huddled group of buildings on the edge of a steep hill.

Unlike the other ruins they'd seen on this part of the island, these had been restored. A crowd was milling around in an open-air courtyard, bouncing along to the calypso music played by a band under a roofed shelter. Mark handed Ellie a plastic cup of bright red liquid. One sniff told her it was rather toxic rum punch, and she sipped it slowly as she swayed to the rounded notes of the steel drums.

Oh, this was better than fancy-pants cooking and business talk. This was just what she'd needed. She looked at Mark, who was sipping his own punch and smiling at her. How had he known?

'Come on,' he said, putting his cup down on a low wall and holding out his hand.

Ellie shook her head. 'I'm a terrible dancer—really clumsy.' Especially these days, when remembering her left from her right was a monumental effort.

'Nobody cares,' Mark said, nodding towards the more exuberant members of the crowd, who'd obviously been enjoying the punch and were flinging their arms and legs around with abandon. 'You can't look any worse than they do.'

She put her cup down too, laughing. 'I can't argue with that,' she said, and he led her to the uneven dusty ground that served as a dance floor.

Ellie discovered that she loved dancing like this. There were no rules, no steps to remember; she just moved her body any way that felt right. And, unsurprisingly, that involved being in close contact with Mark. He hadn't let go of her hand since he'd led her to the dance floor, and she gripped it firmly, determined not to let it slip from between her fingers again.

As they danced, Mark manoeuvred them further away from the main buildings and towards a low wall. After a rather nifty spin Ellie stopped in her tracks, causing Mark to bump softly into her.

'Wow!'

'Told you it was the best place on the island,' Mark said, as Ellie just stared at the scene in front of her.

The view was stupendous. The sun was low on the horizon, and the undulating hills and coastline were drenched in soft, warm colours. Ellie recognised this view as the one they always stuck on the tourist brochures for Antigua. It had to be the most beautiful place in the whole world. She moved forward to rest her hands on the wall, unaware for a moment that Mark hadn't moved away and that her back was being heated by his chest.

'Will you take a photo of us?'

Ellie looked round to see a sweet young redhead with an English accent holding a camera hopefully towards her. She was standing with a lanky guy in long shorts and rather loud, touristy shirt.

She shrugged and smiled back. 'Okay. Sure.'

The girl beamed at her, handed the camera over, then snuggled up to the violent shirt. 'It's our honeymoon,' she explained, glancing adoringly at him.

'Congratulations,' Mark said from behind her, and Ellie became aware of a slow heat building where their bodies were still in contact.

'You've had the same idea as us, I see,' the girl babbled. 'Get here early to get a good view of the sunset. It's our last night and we've watched every one. We're hoping we'll get to see the green flash before we go home.'

Ellie held the camera up and snapped a picture of them grinning toothily at her.

'Green flash?' she said as she handed the camera back to the redhead.

'It's a rare sight,' the woman said as she checked the photo on the screen and smiled. 'Sometimes, when the last part of the sun dips into the sea, you can see a flash of green light as it disappears.'

Loud Shirt Guy nodded. 'Atmospheric conditions have to be just right. It's all to do with astronomical refraction and—'

His wife laid a hand on his arm and he stopped talking. 'Don't bore them with all that, darling,' she said, laughing. Then she whispered behind her hand at Ellie, 'Honestly, he's a scientist, and sometimes he just doesn't know when to stop.'

Ellie could *feel* Mark smiling behind her. Although how you could tell someone was smiling only by being in contact with their chest she wasn't sure.

'Anyway, we're not watching it for the physics, are we, Anton?'

Anton shook his head, and got a misty look in his eyes. 'Island folklore has it that couples who see it together are guaranteed true love.'

A pang of incredible sadness hit Ellie right from out of nowhere. This couple were so sweet. She remembered being that besotted with someone, sure she was going to have a long and happy future with him. She almost wanted to go and give them both a great big hug, to whisper in their ears never to take the time they had together for granted, never to waste even a second. Instead she smiled at them, feeling her eyes fill a little.

'Well, I hope you see it—and congratulations again.'

They nodded their thanks and turned to watch the sun, now dipping dangerously close to the clean line of the ocean. More people were wandering over to watch the sunset and Mark tugged Ellie's arm, leading her down a path, away from the crowd. The view wasn't quite so breathtaking here, but it was framed by trees and she relished not being hemmed in by lots of people, free to feel all the emotions washing over her without being watched. Her fingers crept up to the locket round her neck and she stroked it as she watched the sun go down.

Somehow Mark had hold of her hand again, and he stood beside her, warming her with his mere presence.

Slowly the air grew thick and silence fell as everyone further up the path concentrated on the wavering orange disc that was now dipping itself into the horizon. Ellie didn't move. She hardly dared breathe as she watched the sun inch its way down.

She hadn't thought it possible, just a few short months ago, that she could love again. But here she was, watching the most mesmerising sunset she'd ever seen, with a man who had turned all her rigid expectations on their heads. But did he feel the same way? Was it even possible this was more than a passing attraction for him? She wanted to believe that the look she'd seen on his face in the car was the truth, but she just didn't trust her instincts any more.

A wayward curl blew across her face and she

brushed it away so she could stare harder at the setting sun. He was here with her now, and that was what mattered. Who said love lasted for ever, anyway? She knew better than most that you had to grab the moment while you could. Maybe it was time just to 'go with the flow', as Sam had always encouraged her—as she had been doing when she'd danced to the hypnotic calypso music. Maybe it was time to let life feel something other than small again, no matter what that meant. No matter if *for ever* wasn't part of the package.

Mark leaned forward and whispered in her ear. 'Look.'

The sun was almost gone now, the very last traces only just visible, and she'd been so busy daydreaming she'd almost missed it. Why was it so difficult to live in the moment and not get distracted by wounds of the past or fears for the future? She concentrated hard on the sun, knowing that capturing this moment for her memory banks was important somehow.

And then it happened.

Just as the orange lip of the sun disappeared there was a sizzle of emerald on the horizon. Ellie froze. It lasted only a second or two and then faded away. Mark was standing slightly to the side and behind her. She could hear his breathing, soft and shallow, in her right ear.

Then he began to move, and she moved too, turning to face him.

He looked at her for a long time, a solemn, almost sad expression on his face, and then, just as her mind started to go wild with questions, he leaned in close and kissed her, silencing them all.

Later that evening Ellie wandered on to her veranda alone. She leant on the criss-cross wooden railing and stared in amazement at the confusion of stars jostling for space in the midnight sky. Light from Mark's cabin, a short distance through the gardens, was casting a faint glow on the waving palms, but there was no sign of him.

It had been a magical night—starting with *that* kiss.

By the time they'd returned the short distance up the trail from where they'd watched the sunset the sky had been a velvety dark blue, the sun long disappeared. They'd danced to the steel band, eaten sticky barbecue food with their fingers, and hadn't been able to stop smiling at each other.

Her relationship with Mark had definitely crossed into new territory, but neither of them had brought the subject up, preferring just to live in the moment, rather than spoil it with words and theories.

She wasn't just a fling to him.

The knowledge was there, deep down in her heart—in the same way she'd known after that first day of primary school that Sam's life and hers would always be joined somehow.

There was something between them—her and Mark—something real. Only she didn't have the words to describe it. And for the first time in a very long while the fact she couldn't find the right word, couldn't label something instantly, didn't bother her in the slightest.

The next few days were almost too much for Ellie's mind to deal with. She'd been so accustomed to guilt and pain and misery, clanging round her ankles like shackles, that the light, airy happiness she was feeling took a bit of getting used to. And the glorious island she was on and the wonderful man she was with just made life seem even more surreal.

But who needed real life, anyway?

She'd rather live this dream, where she spent almost every waking moment with Mark. They'd eaten at the most amazing places, ranging from surfside shacks to exclusive restaurants. They'd been sailing and had walked across countless beaches. Some evenings they'd gone out into the bustle of nearby St John's; sometimes they'd just found somewhere quiet to watch the sun set. They hadn't seen the green flash again, but Ellie didn't worry about that. Once must be enough, surely?

And Mark…

He astounded her. He knew her every mood, anticipated her every need. He knew when to hold her tight and when to give her space without her even having to try and get the jumble of an explanation past her lips.

Marrying up this version of Mark with the grinning playboy she'd seen on the television all those months ago was almost impossible. She'd been so blinkered. But, even so, she was sure the way he was behaving wasn't something she'd conveniently blocked out. He was different. More free. He was changing too.

And it only meant she loved him more.

As the week wore on, she felt the shadow of the approaching anniversary looming close on her horizon. With that blocking her view of the sun, it was hard to think about where her relationship with Mark might go, what it would become when they flew home on Saturday.

She'd just have to get Friday out of the way first. Then she'd be able to think clearly. Then maybe, when the plane took off and she watched the ground drop away, the houses and cars all become miniature versions of themselves, she'd be able to leave her small life behind her once and for all.

CHAPTER TEN

MARK finally spotted her, walking down near the shoreline, kicking the wavelets with a half-hearted foot. He walked to the edge of his veranda and focused more carefully, just to make sure he was right. He was. It was Ellie, looking very much like a lost soul on the deserted beach.

A storm had passed over the night before, and he'd lain awake in the early hours, listening to the creaking of his wooden cabin as the rain had gusted against it, the rustling of the tall palms in the hotel gardens as they curved and swayed in the wind, wondering if Ellie was awake in her cabin too. This morning it was grey, and slightly overcast, but everything was clean and fresh and new.

Normally that was a good thing.

He watched Ellie as she turned to face the wind and stared out to sea, lifeless as a statue. Yesterday he'd thought all his prayers had been answered.

Her smiles across the dinner table had been warm and sweet and just for him.

As they'd headed home the sky had darkened, and by midnight rain had been hurling itself out of the sky with the force that only a tropical storm could manage. He and Ellie had spent their time snuggled up on the sofa in his cabin, watching a bad action movie. He couldn't remember the last time he'd had so much fun.

Yet there had been no glitzy nightclub, no suffocating shirt and tie, no polished mannequin on his arm, laughing on cue at his jokes. Just him and Ellie having a late-night Room Service picnic on the carpet in front of the television. They'd talked about anything and everything, and sometimes nothing at all.

His celebrity-hungry girlfriends would have balked at such an evening. There was no point going out with Mark Wilder unless you were going to be *seen* out with him—and it had better be somewhere expensive! They would certainly have frowned upon scanning the film credits for the most interesting-sounding bit part. Ellie had won with 'second tramp in explosion'. It had beaten his 'teenager with nose-stud' hands down.

Relaxing on the sofa with Ellie snuggled up

under his arm, he'd realised that this was what *normal* felt like. He liked it. In fact, he could see himself doing it for a long time to come with her, and he hardly remembered why he had been so terrified of it for almost a decade. Now he had tasted it he wasn't sure he could go back to living without it. It was kind of addictive.

What did that mean?

He tried not to think of the 'm' word, but no matter how he diverted his thoughts they kept swerving back to images of Ellie, dressed in white, a serene smile on her face as he slid a delicate gold band on her finger.

The wind ruffled his hair and his daydreams scattered like the bulbous clouds hurrying towards the skyline. Overnight something had happened. This morning she was withdrawn. No smiles. No bubbling laughter. Today, he hardly existed.

He kicked the railing of the veranda hard. Which was a big mistake—he had bare feet.

What was going on with her? Had she finally taken a good look at him and decided there was nothing more than schmooze and show? Hadn't he criticised himself enough in recent months for the lack of substance in his life?

He raised his foot, ready to take another kick,

but thought better of it. Instead he turned and walked through the cabin to his bedroom to get dressed. It was time to find out what was going on, whether the last few days had just been a mirage or not.

Five minutes later he felt the wet sand caving under the weight of his heels as he strode across the almost deserted beach. Ellie was now only a billowing speck in the distance. A remnant of last night's wind lifted her loose skirt as she wandered along the shoreline.

He lengthened his stride.

She didn't hear him come up behind her. She was busy drawing in the wet sand with a long stick. He didn't want to startle her, so he stopped a few feet away and spoke her name so gently it was only just audible above the splash of the waves near their feet.

She stopped tracing a large letter 'C' in the damp sand. Mark's heart pounded like the waves on the distant rocks as he waited for her response. Her head lifted first, but her eyes remained fixed on her sandy scrawlings a few seconds longer before she found the courage to meet his enquiring gaze. The rims of her eyes were pink and moist.

Any words he'd had ready dissolved in the back

of his throat. Devoid of anything sensible to say, he held out the single pink rose he'd lifted from the vase in his room. Ellie started to reach for it, then her face crumpled and silent tears overflowed down her cheeks. He dropped the rose and stepped towards her, intent on gathering her up in his arms, but could only watch in horror as she buckled and sat weeping in the sand.

'Ellie? Ellie, what is it?'

He sank down next to her and pulled her firmly into his arms. She tried to answer him, but her words were swallowed in another round of stomach-wrenching sobs. So he waited. He held her and he waited. Waited until the tide turned and the hot flood of tears became a damp trickle. She pushed away from his chest and stood up, shaking the sand from her skirt.

Her voice wobbled. 'I'm sorry.'

Mark leapt to his feet and reached for her.

'Don't be.' He pulled her close to his chest and stroked her wind-ruffled hair. 'Is there something I can do?'

She swept her fingers over her damp eyes and straightened, seeming to have made a decision about something. 'I need to tell you something…' She took a deep breath and held it. 'It's the anniversary today. Four years since…since Sam and Chloe died.'

Her hand automatically reached for the silver locket she always wore. Mark didn't need to be told what pictures it held. He'd had an inkling, but now he knew for sure.

He didn't say anything. What could he say that wouldn't sound patronising or trite? So he just continued to hold her, love her, and hoped that would be enough.

'I didn't mean to shut you out or push you away,' she said. 'I just needed some time to think. It's different this year. So much has happened in the last few months…'

Slowly she unclipped the flat oval face of the locket and showed its contents to him. On one side was a little girl—blonde curls like her mother, as cute as a button. On the other side a sandy-haired man, with an infectious grin and a gleam of love in his eyes for whomever had been taking the photo. It was hard to look at the pictures, because it made him scared that she wasn't ready to move on, but he appreciated what a big step it had been for her to show him.

Ellie stooped to pick up the discarded rose and peeled the crushed outer petals off to reveal undamaged ones underneath. Mark felt ill. What if she was still in love with her dead husband? And how horrible was he for being jealous of him? He was polluting the pure emotions Ellie had provoked in him by thinking this way.

'It was the rose that set me off,' she said, picking up the bud and bringing it to her nose. 'Pink was Chloe's favourite colour.'

He almost thought the conversation was going to end there, the gap was so long, but just when he'd decided she'd lapsed back into silence she continued.

'I didn't get to go to the funeral—I was only barely conscious, couldn't walk, couldn't talk—but my mother showed me the pictures. She thought it would help. Maybe it did.'

She broke off to look out to sea again.

'Chloe had a tiny white coffin with silver handles, and Mum had chosen a wreath made only of pink roses that covered it completely. I planted a bush in the cemetery for her when I got out of hospital.'

Mark felt moisture threaten his own eyelids. She reached out and touched his cheek, stroking it with the fleshy pad of her thumb. 'Thank you for coming to find me. Thank you for never telling me how *lucky* I was to survive. You have no idea how much that means to me.'

How did she do it? How did she think beyond herself so easily? She had every right to spend the day cut off from the world, wallowing as much as she wanted. Ellie had lost part of her life to a fog her brain had created. What must it be like to not have been able to go to the funerals? To never get closure? Part of her must yearn to remember something from those days.

In contrast, he was a coward. He'd *chosen* to forget Helena, forget about love and commitment. And that hadn't helped him heal either. If anything it had just made him more shallow, less brave.

He gazed into her beautiful damp eyes. The pale green was even more vivid against their slightly pink tinge, and he caught her face in his palms.

'You're amazing, Ellie Bond.'

She lowered her lids. 'I don't *feel* very amazing. I've spent the last few years feeling terrified mostly, and recently—' She looked back at him. The warmth in her weak smile quickened his pulse. 'Recently I've just felt plain old crazy.'

'How can you say that?'

Her lashes lowered and she gave a derisive

laugh. 'I would have thought our first meeting would have been ample proof!'

He smiled. 'I think that, despite first impressions, you're probably the sanest person I know. At least you know what's real—what's important. I'd forgotten.'

That made her smile, the thought that someone else might have to wrestle with their memories too, that she wasn't entirely alone in that predicament. Their lips met briefly, tenderly. He could taste the salt from her tears.

'How you survived what you went through I'll never know. Lesser women would have crumbled.'

'But I did crumble. That is until I met—' she stopped and swallowed '—you.' Her voice dropped to a whisper. 'I'd forgotten how wonderful life could be.'

'I still think you're pretty amazing.' He held her close and his words drifted softly into her ear. 'You don't see it in yourself. That's one of the reasons why I love you.'

She froze in his arms and Mark's stomach churned. Ellie pulled back slightly and scrutinised his face, analysing his expression. He willed his facial muscles to keep still, however much they wanted to collapse. He hadn't a clue what she could see in his face. Honesty, he hoped. All he was aware of was the slicing agony as he waited for her to say something. Anything...

A couple more seconds and he was going to scream.

She blinked away a fresh tear. 'You—you love me?'

Mark recognised that feeling he got in dreams, when he suddenly discovered he'd been walking down the street naked and everybody knew it but him. The familiar urge to bolt was so strong he could taste it. In response, he ground his heels a little deeper into the sand as an anchor.

'Yes. I do. I love you.'

Just as he thought he was going to suffocate on the tension-thick atmosphere Ellie launched herself into his arms and covered his face with a hundred little kisses. At first he couldn't move. He hardly dared ask himself what this meant, hardly dared to hope.

What was that sound?

She was laughing. In between kisses, she was laughing! That was all he needed. He hugged her so tight her feet lifted off the floor. Their lips sought each other out and he lost all sense of reality for a while. When they finally pulled themselves apart rays of sunlight were punching holes in the gruff clouds. He looked at her face, alive with joy, such a difference from the mournful expression she'd worn when he'd first found her. Tears still followed the damp tracks down her cheeks, but he hoped for a very different reason.

At that moment he knew he wanted to love her so completely, so thoroughly, that every speck of pain would be soothed, every wound healed. He might not be able to change her past, but he was going to make darn sure her future was filled with all the adoration and happiness he could give her. He felt strangely unafraid at the thought of for ever.

He linked his fingers in between hers and they strolled back along the shoreline. Every now and then he would spot one of Ellie's random sand doodles. He knew now that the 'C' had been for Chloe. The selfish part of him dreaded seeing a letter 'S'. But he hadn't—yet. Only some squiggles, her name and a flower.

There was another one up ahead he couldn't quite discern. He strained his eyes, trying to read it upside down. When he eventually made it out his heart nearly stopped.

It was an 'M', encased in a gently curving heart.

The words were out of his mouth before his brain had a chance to intervene.

'Marry me?'

What had he just said?

There must still be static left in the air from the storm, because she felt tiny electric charges detonate all over her body. Then a sick feeling of disappointment hit her in the pit of her stomach. She'd heard him say something like this before. She yanked her hand out of his. How could he ruin the moment like this?

'Don't joke with me, Mark.' If he was bright, he'd heed the steely warning hidden in her reply. She turned to face him, expecting to see the trademark grin across his big smart mouth, but it wasn't there.

Another jolt of electricity hit her.

'You're serious, aren't you?'

He scooped her into his arms and kissed her until she nearly forgot the subject of this surreal conversation. Nearly.

'Of course I'm serious!'

She didn't know whether to laugh or cry. Mark started to kiss her again, but she stepped back, holding him at bay.

'Hang on a second, Mark. I can't think straight

when you're that close.' She'd thought he'd laugh, but he didn't. She smoothed her wind-blown hair and turned a slow circle in the sand, scanning the horizon for an answer. He came up behind her and hugged her close, his warmth delicious against her cool skin.

'What's there to think about? I love you. Don't you love me?'

'Mark, it's not that easy!'

He nuzzled in close to her neck. 'It could be.'

Could it? Could happiness really be that easy? It was as if someone had told her it was okay to reach out and grab the stars if she wanted to.

For four long years she'd been living in the past. Trying to remember… Trying to forget… Recently she'd actually managed to live in the present, enjoy the moment. But did that mean she was ready to think about the future? That was something she hadn't done for such a long time, she realised, for all her big talk about 'breaking free'. She hadn't really been looking forward when she'd taken the job as Mark's housekeeper; she'd been looking back over her shoulder, running away from ghosts.

But now, standing here on this beach, she was starting to think that the future might be wonderful instead of scary. Today she'd found some peace. And Mark was a wonderful man, so much more than he gave himself credit for. Maybe it *was* that easy. Maybe this was one impulse she should follow one hundred percent, because, boy, she really wanted to say yes.

He turned her to face him without breaking contact, keeping her in the protective circle of his arms. 'Ellie. I love you. I've never felt this way about anyone. Ever. I can't imagine spending another second of my life without you.' In a solemn gesture he took her hands in his, kissed them and lowered himself onto one knee.

Now she knew she really was dreaming! There was no way this could be happening to her. Still, she hoped the alarm clock wasn't going to go off any time soon.

The earnest look on his face made her eyes sting again. 'Ellie Bond, will you do me the honour of becoming my wife?'

She could feel his whole body shaking as she lowered herself to sit on his raised knee and kissed him sweetly, passionately.

'Is that a *yes*?'

Her breath warmed his earlobe as she whispered, 'Yes.'

Mark's ferocious kiss destroyed their precarious balancing act and they both fell onto the sand, tangled but still joined at the lips. Ellie wasn't sure how long they stayed there 'celebrating'. Long enough for the tide to creep in a bit further and take a peek.

'Mark, my feet are getting wet.'

'Do you care?'

'Not really.'

More jubilant celebrations.

By the time the salty water was lapping at the hem of her skirt she surrendered.

'We can't stay here all day, you know.'

Mark fell back into the sand and stared at the vivid blue sky. 'Shame. I was hoping we could just float away to a desert island and never be heard of again.'

That night at dinner they suddenly remembered they needed to think practicalities if they were really serious about getting married.

'What sort of wedding do you want?' Mark asked Ellie as she dug into her creamy dessert, desperately hoping it wouldn't be the three-ring circus Helena had insisted on. Weddings like that felt like bad omens.

Ellie swallowed her mouthful and thought for a

moment. 'Something simple.' She dug her spoon into the coconut and rum thing again, but it stopped halfway to her mouth and hovered there, threatening to drop its contents back into the bowl while she considered his question further. 'Something small…private. Just you and me on a sunny day, somewhere beautiful.'

That gave him an idea. 'Somewhere like here?'

Ellie put her spoon back in the bowl and smiled at him. 'That would be perfect! You mean come back in a few months?'

That was exactly what he'd been thinking. But then he thought about all the to-ing and fro-ing, all the hideous preparations and tensions in the run-up to a wedding. That would just spoil everything, ruin the atmosphere of perfection that was clinging to them at the moment.

'How about we get married here? Now. In a few days.' He looked at her earnestly. 'As soon as possible.'

She opened and closed her mouth. Then she made that scrunched-up face she always did when she was trying to process something unexpected.

'We'll have a big party for friends and family when we get back home,' he added. Ellie looked horrified, and Mark remembered the last party at

Larkford. He took hold of her hand. '*Real* friends only, I promise.'

'This isn't another one of what *you* think are your hilarious jokes, is it?'

He was deadly serious. How did he make her see that?

'Ellie, I've been hiding for too long, waiting for too long.' He watched as the tension eased from her face and she smiled at him, nodding in agreement. He stopped smiling and looked straight into her eyes. 'I don't want to wait any more.'

She let out a happy sigh. 'Mark, you're asking the right girl, then—because I have this horrible impulse to go along with anything you say, and I just can't be bothered to fight it.'

Ellie stared at herself in the bathroom mirror.

'I'm getting married tomorrow!' she screamed at the idiot grinning back at her. Then she screamed again, just because it was fun. Oh, get a grip, girl! You can't just stand here all day smiling at yourself. You've got some serious shopping to do today. And a fiancé to corner before he disappeared off to do whatever secret things he'd planned and wouldn't tell her about.

One more grin in the mirror for luck, and then

she ran out of her bathroom and got dressed in the first things she found in the wardrobe.

The last few days had been madness. Her cheeks hurt from smiling so much. She'd thought she would be flying home days ago, but she was still here in paradise with Mark, and things were going to get even more perfect. She couldn't think about anything else. Her mind just refused to prise itself from that track and she wasn't inclined to let it.

Of course a voice in the back of her head whispered to her, asking her if this was all too quick, asking whether there was unfinished business she needed to sort out first. But she didn't want to listen to that voice, so she drowned it out with a slightly off-key rendition of 'Oh, What a Beautiful Morning'.

Happiness was within her grasp, here and now. She was going to snatch it before the whole dream disappeared in a puff of smoke. No more fear. No more trepidation. Just facing the future with Mark at her side.

But what about the past? the voice said. *What are you going to do with that?*

Ellie belted out the chorus of the song and ran through the garden. She burst through the unlocked doors of Mark's cabin like a miniature whirlwind.

He was in the sitting room, poring over some faxes. His face lit up as he saw her. 'Good morning. And what have you come as today?'

'Huh?' Ellie stopped and looked down, then burst into laughter as she took in her floaty floral-print blouse and her pyjama bottoms.

'I had other things on my mind while I was getting dressed,' she admitted with a wry smile.

'Pyjama bottoms…hmm…' Mark claimed his morning kiss. 'They remind me of the first time we met,' he said, making a feather-soft trail from her neck to her ear.

Ellie flung her arms around him. 'If you really want to recreate our first meeting I think we need to be a little more—how shall I put it?—horizon-tal,' she said, and let her weight fall backwards, pulling them both down onto the large sofa behind her. 'And you! You should be wearing consider-ably less!'

'You know I'm not that sort of girl,' he quipped. 'I thought I'd made it very clear. You have to sign on the dotted line before you get to sample the goods.'

'Spoilsport!'

'Only twenty hours to go. Surely you can wait that long?'

'Only just.' She pulled him close for another

kiss. 'Just a deposit,' she assured him, making sure she got her money's worth. Both sets of parents and Ellie's brother were due to fly in for the wedding, so they'd planned a meal at the hotel after the ceremony. 'Do we have to stay through *all* of the wedding breakfast? Can't we leave early?'

Mark threw his head back and laughed. He pressed his lips against her forehead as he untangled himself and stood up. 'We won't have to stay long.'

'Five minutes?'

'Three at the most.'

It was her turn to laugh. He walked back to the desk. 'Now, as for the rest of today, you have to go shopping. You can't get married in another outfit like that. Carla, the stylist from the shoot, has faxed me a list of shops in St John's that you can visit for a dress. Thank goodness Antiguan red tape is just as laid-back and flexible as everything else on this island, and I can go and pick up the marriage licence today, once some essential documents have arrived. And, talking of essential elements of our wedding, I have one last surprise for you.'

He grabbed her hand and dragged her with him to another cabin. When they got onto the white-painted veranda he gave her a little nudge in the

direction of the open door. Ellie gave him a quiz-
zical look, then stepped inside.

'Charlie!'

Charlie jumped off the sofa and bounced over to
Ellie, squealing, and dragged her fully inside the
cabin. Then she flung her arms around Ellie's neck
and yelled her congratulations in her ear. Ellie was
already having trouble catching her breath, and
Charlie's bear hug left her practically airless. She
patted her friend's back in a pathetic attempt to
return the gesture.

'I don't understand. What are you doing here?'

'Do you think I'd miss this? Mark called me the
day before yesterday, broke the news, and asked
me to fly over with birth certificates and such. I'm
a rather stunning, elegant, designer-clad courier!'
She did a little twirl just to prove it.

Ellie grinned. 'You're more than that! And the
first thing you can do to make up for almost giving
me a heart attack is to come dress shopping. It's
the least my bridesmaid can do.'

Charlie's high-pitched squeal almost shredded
Ellie's eardrums.

Sunrise.

Ellie and Mark walked towards the minister arm

in arm as the sun lifted above the horizon. She loved Mark for suggesting her favourite time of day for the wedding. There was something so pure and fresh about the early-morning sun. And it was a beautiful symbol for her life. A fresh start, new hope. Light and warmth where she'd thought there could only be darkness.

Her bare feet sank into the cool, silky sand as they passed the few guests up early to share the ceremony. Charlie and Kat, who'd insisted on cancelling something important to be there, stood beside the minister in their bridesmaids' outfits, smiling at Mark and Ellie as they approached. Charlie looked as if she'd already had to break out the emergency hanky. It was just as well Ellie had insisted she wear waterproof mascara.

Ellie took a deep breath and looked down at her feet. Her softly flowing white chiffon dress was blowing gently round her ankles. Her feet looked almost as creamy as the pale sand. Her toenails were painted a shade of deep pink to match the exotic blooms woven into her hair and in her bouquet. And on her left foot was a white gold toe-ring, beautiful in its simplicity. Mark's gift to her this morning. Just until they got a proper engagement ring, he'd said. But she didn't care; she thought it was perfect.

She wore no other jewellery. Not even her locket. Much as she loved it, she couldn't wear it any more—especially not today. It wouldn't be fair to Mark.

As they reached the minister they halted and turned to face each other. How could she be this lucky? Finding love once with Sam had been wonderful enough, but finding it with Mark was a miracle. She never thought she'd have a second chance. She was so thankful he'd made her see that happiness didn't always come in identically shaped packages.

She almost didn't hear the minister as he started the ceremony, she was so busy staring at Mark. She'd never seen him looking so devastatingly handsome. Her eyes never left him throughout the vows. They might as well have been standing on the beach alone for all she knew. Finally she heard the words *husband and wife*, and the minister gave Mark permission to kiss the bride.

She should have known from the naughty grin on his face that he was up to no good. He lingered a little longer than propriety suggested on the kiss, then swept her up into his arms, hooked one arm under her knees and headed off down the beach with her, leaving her dress billowing behind them and the small band of guests open-mouthed.

'Mark!' she gasped, when he'd gone a dozen or so steps. 'Where are you going? We've still got the reception to get through!'

He slowed to a halt. 'I thought you wanted to disappear as soon as possible after the wedding?'

'I'm tempted, believe me, but we can't leave our guests waiting.'

'Just for you,' he said, and let her legs glide down to meet the sand, then kissed the tip of her nose. Laughing, they walked back to the small group of guests, who were sharing indulgent smiles.

By the time they congregated in the hotel gardens under a flower-draped pergola for their celebratory feast, the sun was glowing gold and fully above the horizon. The hotel chef had been very inventive with the food, and a stunning array of mouthwatering dishes was ready for them. Since the numbers were small they all sat around one large table, sipping champagne and chatting.

After they had eaten, made the toasts and cut the cake, Kat surprised them by picking up her guitar, which had been cleverly hidden behind a planter, and proceeded to serenade them with a song especially composed for the occasion. Tears welled in Ellie's eyes as she listened to the beautiful lyrics.

All my tomorrows are nothing but yours, all my yesterdays my gift to you.

It was the best wedding present anyone could have given them. The chorus stuck in her mind, and she found she was humming it as they prepared to leave for the honeymoon.

'Where are we going, then?' Ellie asked, puzzled, as Mark led her not to the front of the hotel, as she'd expected, but on to the beach. Mark just smiled an infuriating smile that said *you'll see*.

A small speedboat, with a satin ribbon tied bridal-car fashion on the front, was sitting a few feet from the shoreline.

'I thought we'd float away to that desert island we talked about and never be heard of again,' he said, as he lifted her into his arms once again and waded out to deposit her in the boat.

CHAPTER ELEVEN

MARK was as good as his word, Ellie thought, as she rolled sleepily over in bed. Two weeks on their very own private tropical island had been absolute bliss. She snuggled back against him. A heavy arm draped over her waist and his breaths were long and even. Heaven.

The villa they were staying in was small, but luxurious. The local owners brought fresh food and supplies every day, but were discreet enough that Ellie had not caught sight of them yet. She found enough lazy energy to smile as she remembered how Mark had laughed when she had referred to them as the 'shopping fairies'.

If only they could stay here for ever. But today was their last day. Tomorrow it was back to England. She frowned, and snuggled even further into Mark's sleeping body. The last couple of weeks had been like a wonderful dream and she wasn't sure she was ready for the cold grey slap of reality yet. Here they were just Mark and Ellie, besotted newlyweds. No labels, no outside expectations, free to be themselves. The thought of going home made her shiver. She loved Mark desperately, but she had an inkling that getting used to being Mrs Wilder was going to take some effort.

Warm golden light filtered through the sheer curtains. She guessed the sun had been up a while; it was maybe nine or ten o' clock. Her tummy rumbled in confirmation. No wonder! Their half-eaten dinner still lay on the dining table, abandoned in favour of traditional honeymoon recreation.

Wonderful as it is, lying here tangled with my husband, a girl's gotta eat!

She wriggled out from under his arm and reached for her robe. Thankfully she had managed to buy something a little more appropriate for a new bride than her old ratty pink one. The ancient garment certainly didn't come under the category of *sexy honeymoon lingerie.* She'd been astonished when Mark had seemed disappointed she hadn't packed it. Weird. She slung the wisp of ivory silk over her shoulders, only bothering with it because she was afraid of running into the 'fairies'. She left it unfastened and walked away from the bed. A sudden jerk of the sash trailing behind her arrested her progress.

A sleepy voice mumbled from under a pillow, 'Don't go. Come back to bed.'

'I'll be back in a sec. I'm starving!'

'So am I.'

She laughed. 'Why don't I think you've got breakfast on your mind?'

A naughty chuckle from under the pillow told her she was spot-on. In a moment of feminine contrariness she decided to make him wait, and continued her journey to the kitchen. The sash pulled taut as he tried to stop her, but the slippery silk whooshed through the loops and she disappeared out through the door. She laughed gently as she imagined what he must look like with the sash dangling uselessly from his outstretched hand.

'Ellie?' he yelled from the bedroom.

She was still smiling as she reached into the fridge for the jug of fresh orange juice. 'Sorry. Forgot what you said. You'll just have to wait,' she called back, pleased with her own self-mockery.

Mark's effort at secretive footsteps was atrocious, but she pretended not to hear him and readied herself for his attack. She detected a flicking movement out of the corner of her eye, and before she could work out what it was her missing sash looped over her head and dragged her backwards into the hard wall of his chest.

His voice was very nearly a growl. 'I said, Don't go!'

'Mark! I just spilled orange juice all over myself.' She looked down and watched a bead of liquid travel down her torso towards her belly button.

He loosened the sash just enough to let her turn to face him. 'We'll just have to clean it up, then, won't we?' he said, a truly wicked glint in his eyes.

Ellie sighed as he started tugging her back towards the bedroom. She was pretty sure he wasn't going to fetch a towel.

Ellie wandered outside and sank her feet into the dewy grass. The vibrant green carpet welcomed her feet and she sighed. It was wonderful to be home. She might have lived on in the cottage after Sam and Chloe had gone, but it turned from a home to a shell of bricks and mortar the day they died. She turned and looked at the majestically crumbling manor house. Larkford Place felt like home—but then she'd feel at home in a caravan if Mark was there.

She was surprised at how easy the transition had

been. She'd been so worried that she would feel different when they returned from the Caribbean. Over three weeks later she still felt alarmingly peaceful. She'd experienced a strange sense of foreboding on the flight home, but if trouble was looming in the distance it was hiding itself round a dimly lit corner.

She looked at the open French windows and wished that Mark would stroll through them any second and join her. The curtains rippled in promise, but she knew he wouldn't appear. He was off on business for a few days and due home first thing tomorrow. She'd had the opportunity to go with him. She'd already travelled with him once since they'd been back, but she'd been feeling a bit below par for a couple of days and had decided to stay home and recharge her batteries while Mark flew to Ireland. The idea of sleeping in her own bed rather than a hotel one, however luxurious the surroundings, was too much of a lure. She took a careful sip of her hot tea.

Yuck!

It tasted awful. The milk must be off. She would just have to make a new one. She walked into the kitchen and poured the rest of her tea down the sink, then put on the kettle for a fresh cup. While she was waiting for it to boil she went in search of the offending milk in the fridge.

A row of unopened bottles stood like pristine soldiers in the door. Where was the one she'd used earlier? She moved a couple of items around on the nearby shelf to see if the half-used bottle was hidden away behind something. Nope. Hang on! What were the teabags doing in here?

Oh, well. She popped open a fresh pint of milk and sniffed it, while keeping her nose as far away as possible. No, this one was fine. Having done that, she made herself another cup of tea and sank into one of the wooden chairs round the table. She took a long sip, scowled, then spat it back into the cup. What was wrong with the tea today? It would have to be orange juice instead. She returned the rather chilly box of tea bags to its proper resting place in the cupboard—or would have done if a bottle of milk hadn't been sitting in its spot.

Obviously her absent-minded tendencies were getting worse. She'd been under the mistaken impression she'd been improving recently, but she was clearly deluded. She laughed quietly to herself as she returned the milk to the fridge.

Then she fell silent. These weren't her normal

memory lapses. This was something new. Should she be worried about that? She'd never been scatty like this before, unless you counted that time years *before* the accident when…

Oh, my!

Ellie continued staring into the open fridge, the cool air making no impact on her rapidly heating face. When she let go of the door and let it slam closed she realised her hands were shaking. She sat back down at the table, her thirst forgotten, and tried to assemble all the evidence in her cluttered brain. The milk, the tea, the lack of energy—it was all falling into place.

She'd completely gone off both tea and coffee when she'd been carrying Chloe—hadn't even been able to stand the smell when Sam had opened a jar of instant coffee to make himself one. She'd made him drink it in the garden! And then she'd developed an overwhelming craving for tinned pineapple sprinkled liberally with pepper.

Her palm flattened over her stomach. She stood up, then sat down again.

I can't be pregnant! Not already.

She hadn't even considered the possibility, although it would certainly explain her sudden lethargy. A creeping nausea rose in her throat, but she was sure it was more a result of shock than morning sickness.

How could this have happened?

Er…stupid question, Ellie! You spent more time with your clothes off than on on honeymoon. Yes, they'd been careful, but nothing was guaranteed one hundred percent in this life.

She wasn't sure she was ready to have another baby! Life was changing so fast at the moment she could hardly keep up. She needed to get used to being married before she could consider all the possibilities for the future.

And what was Mark going to say?

She hoped he would be pleased, but what if he wasn't? They hadn't even talked about this stuff yet, having been too caught up in a whirlwind wedding and being newlyweds to think about anything sensible.

Calm down! You're getting ahead of yourself!

She didn't even know if she *was* pregnant yet. All she knew for sure was that she'd had a dodgy cup of tea and had misplaced the milk. She didn't have to turn insignificant minor events into a major crisis, now, did she?

Ellie shook her head. Talk about her imagination running away with her. What she needed to do right now was take a few deep breaths and have a shower. Which was exactly what she did. However, all the time she was washing she couldn't shake the nagging voice in the back of her head.

You can't run away from this one, Ellie. You can't bury your head in the sand. But she hadn't been running away from things recently, had she? She'd run *to* Mark, not away from something else. At least that was how it had felt at the time.

She stepped out of the shower and got dressed. She needed to find out for sure. She'd go down to the chemist in the village and buy a test. Strike that. She'd already got to know the local residents, and if the village drums were doing their usual work the news that she might be expecting would be round the village in a nanosecond. The fact that dashing Mr Wilder had married his house-keeper was still the main topic of local gossip. A baby on the way would be too juicy a titbit for the village grapevine to ignore.

She'd be better off going into town and shopping at one of the large chemists. Much easier to be anonymous then. At least when Mark got home tomorrow she'd have had a chance to absorb the outcome herself.

The thought that the test might be negative

should have made her feel more peaceful. Instead she felt low at the prospect. If the test *was* negative, she would make a light-hearted story of it to tell Mark over dinner tomorrow. She'd tell him how freaked out she'd been, see what his reaction was, test the waters.

Two hours later she was standing in the bathroom, holding the little cellophane-wrapped box as if it was an unexploded bomb.

You're not going to find out by staring at it.

She removed the crinkly wrapping and opened the box. How could something as mundane as a plastic stick turn out to be the knife-edge that her whole life was balanced on? She sat on the closed toilet lid while waiting for the result, the test laid on one thigh. Two minutes to wait. If someone had told her she was only going to live another two minutes, it would seem like a measly amount of time. How, then, could this couple of minutes stretch so far they seemed to be filling the rest of the day?

First the test window. Good. One blue line. It was working. Then wait for the next window. She waited for what seemed an age. Nothing. She stood up, threw the test onto the shelf over the sink and ran out of the room crying.

All that stress for nothing. She ought to be

relieved! It gave her a little more time to think, to plan, to find out what Mark wanted.

Suddenly she wished he was there. She wanted to feel his strong arms wrapped around her, wanted him to hold her tight against his chest and stroke her hair.

She grabbed a wad of tissues from the box beside her bed and blew her nose loudly. She should get out of here, get some fresh air. Perhaps she should pick up the papers from the village shop. Mark liked to read a selection, from the broadsheets to the tabloids, mostly to keep track of what attention his clients were attracting in the press.

She went back to collect the pregnancy test and picked it up, with the intention of putting it in the bin, but the moment she looked at it she dropped it into the sink in shock. The breath left her body as if she'd been slapped with a cricket bat.

The tears must be blurring her vision! She dragged the hem of her T-shirt across her eyes and stared at it again.

Two blue lines?

She took it to the window to get more light. Her eyes weren't deceiving her. Granted, the second one was very faint, compared to the first, but there were definitely two blue lines. The hormones had to be only just detectable. She could hardly believe it, but there it was—in blue and white.

I'm going to have a baby. Our baby.

Suddenly the rambling old house seemed claustrophobic. She needed to get outside, feel the fresh air on her skin. The garden called her, and she ran down to it and kicked her flip-flops off. Her 'engagement' toe-ring glinted in the morning sun as she stepped onto the grass and began to walk.

A stroll through Larkford Place's grounds should have been pleasant in high summer. The far reaches of the garden, unspoilt and untended, were alive with wild flowers, butterflies and buzzing insects. But Ellie noticed none of it. All she could think about was having a little boy, with a shock of thick dark hair like his father and eyes the colour of warm chocolate.

Was this how she'd felt when she'd realised she'd been expecting the last time? It seemed so long ago now, a memory half obscured by the fog of the accident. But her last pregnancy had been planned. This one was…well, a surprise to put it mildly.

She stopped and looked a bright little poppy,

wavering in the breeze. Through the confusion and doubts, joy bubbled up inside her, pushing them aside. She wanted this baby. She already loved this baby—just as much as she'd loved…

Images of golden ringlets and gap-toothed smiles filled her mind, but there was something missing. A word missing.

Her hands, which had been circling her tummy, went still. Just as much as she'd loved…

No. Not now. Not this name. This was one name she was *never* allowed to forget, never allowed to lose. It was too awful. Ellie looked back at the house and began to run.

This couldn't be happening. She couldn't have forgotten her own daughter's name.

Mark burst through the front door with a huge bunch of wilted flowers in his hand. They had looked a bit better before they'd spent two long, sticky hours in the passenger seat of the Aston Martin.

'Ellie?'

No answer. She was probably out in the garden. He almost sprinted into the kitchen. The French windows, her normal escape route, were closed. On closer inspection he discovered they were locked. He ran back to the entrance hall and called her name more loudly. The slight echo from his shout jarred the silence.

Okay, maybe she was out. He was half a day early, after all.

He looked at his watch. Nearly four o'clock. She couldn't be too far away. He'd just go and have a shower, then lie in wait. He chuckled and loosened his tie as he hopped up the stairs two at a time.

But as the afternoon wore on Ellie didn't appear. He ended up in the kitchen, wishing she'd materialise there somehow, and he found her note near the kettle. Well, it wasn't even a proper letter—just a sticky note on the kitchen counter, telling him that she'd gone.

He sat down on one of the chairs by the kitchen table and put his head in his hands.

Not again. She'd seemed so happy since the wedding.

That's when they leave—when they're happy. They don't need you any more.

No. This couldn't happen with Ellie. He loved her too much. More than Helena. So much more. He stood up. He'd be damned if he lost a second wife this way. But if she was really intent on going she bloody well owed him an explanation. He wasn't going to let her waltz off without a backward glance.

* * *

The keys jumped from Ellie's fingers as if they had a life of their own. She muttered through her tears and bent to scoop them up from the front step. Thankfully the holiday company had told her they'd had a cancellation this week. The cottage was empty. Perhaps if she went inside it would help.

Although she'd remembered Chloe's name almost the second she'd reached Larkford's kitchen, she still couldn't shake the clammy, creeping feeling of disloyalty and guilt. She'd needed to come somewhere she could rid herself of this horrible feeling of being disconnected from her past.

She slid the key into the lock and started the familiar routine of pulling and turning to ease it open. It was feeling particularly uncooperative today. She gave the key one last jiggle and felt the levers give. The door creaked open.

For no reason she could think of, she burst into tears.

The cream and terracotta tiled hallway seemed familiar and strange at the same time. The surfaces were cleared of all her knickknacks and photos, but the furniture was still *in situ*. Even devoid of personal items it seemed more welcoming than when she'd left on that grey, rainy day months ago.

Ellie hadn't planned to end up here. She just

had. An impulse. She walked into the sitting room and slumped into her favourite armchair.

I should never have left this chair. I should have stayed here eating biscuits and never gone to Larkford. Then I would never have forgotten you, my darling girl.

But then she wouldn't have this new baby. And she really wanted it. She clamped her hands to her stomach, as if to reassure the tiny life inside, and her eyes glittered with maternal fierceness.

If Mark didn't want it, then she'd just bring it up on her own.

Ellie shook her head. She hadn't even told Mark yet, didn't have a clue what his reaction would be. She was just making the same mistake she always made: an idea had crept into her head and she'd sprinted away with it like an Olympic athlete, not even bothering to check that she was running in the right direction. Maybe she was so terrified of losing Mark that deep down she almost expected something to come along and demolish it. And at the first hint of trouble she'd been only too ready to believe her luck couldn't hold out.

Sitting here moping was doing her no good. She pulled herself to her feet and started to walk round the house. As she visited every room different memories came alive: Chloe riding her truck up and down the hall; Sam marking homework at the dining table; the kitchen counter where she had made cakes with Chloe, more flour down their fronts than in the mixing bowl. And she realised she'd never been able to do this before, never been able to look at her cottage and see it alive with wonderful warm memories of her lost family.

As she sat trying to process all the new information Kat's song from the wedding drifted through her head:

Yesterday is where I live, trapped by ghosts and memories.
But I can't stay frozen, my heart numb, because tomorrow is calling me...

Ellie guessed the song had been about her breakup with Razor, but the simple lyrics about learning to love again had been so right for their wedding day too. 'All My Tomorrows' was the title. And she'd promised the rest of hers to Mark, willingly. Nothing in the world could make her take that promise back. So there was only one thing to do: she had to go back home—her real home, Larkford—and let Mark know he was going to be a father. Whatever fallout happened, happened. They would just have to deal with it together.

Her instincts told her it was going to be okay. She hoped she was brave enough to listen to them.

She grabbed her keys off the table and took long strides into the hall, her eyes fixed on the front door. A shadow crossed the glazed panel. She hesitated, then walked a few steps further, only to halt again as a fist pounded on the door.

'Ellie? Are you there?'

She dropped her keys.

'Ellie!'

'Mark?' Her voice was shaky, but a smile stretched her trembling lips. She ran to the door and pressed her palms against the glass.

'Let me in, or so help me I'm just going to have to break the door down!'

She patted her pockets, then scanned the hallway, remembering she'd dropped her keys. She ran to pick them up, but it took three attempts before her shaking fingers kept a grip on them. As fast as she could she raced back to the door and jammed the key in the lock. An ugly grinding sound followed as she turned it, then the key refused to move any further. She wiggled and jiggled it, pushed and pulled the door, trying all her old tricks, but it wouldn't budge. The key would not turn in either direction, so she couldn't even get it out again to have another go.

'Ellie? Open the door!' The last shred of patience disappeared from his voice.

'I'm trying! The lock's jammed.'

'Let me try.'

The door shuddered and groaned under Mark's assault, but remained stubbornly firm.

Ellie sighed. 'They don't make doors like this any more.'

Between pants, she heard Mark mutter, 'You're telling me.'

She pressed her face to the stained glass design, able to see him through a clear piece of glass in the centre. He looked tired, disheveled and incredibly sexy. Without warning, she started to cry again.

He stopped wrestling with the door and looked at her through the textured glass. 'We have to talk.'

She gulped. He sounded serious. Was serious good or bad? Good. Serious was good. Please God, let serious be good!

'I know,' she said.

'Why are you here, instead of at home?'

She took a deep breath and turned away from

him, pressed her back against the door, then slid to the floor.

'How did you know where to find me?'

'I phoned Charlie in a panic and she suggested I might find you here. I'd already been to your parents' house and your brother's.'

She nodded. Charlie knew her so well. Maybe too well. If her friend hadn't guessed where she was she might have made it back to Larkford and Mark would never have known how stupid she'd been this afternoon. But why had her first impulse been to run? To come here? Did that mean something?

'Ellie?'

She took a deep breath. 'Do you think we got married too fast, Mark? I mean, did we get carried away? Should we have waited?' Everything just seemed so confusing today.

She heard him sit on the step. His feet scraped the gravel path as he stretched his legs out. 'Are you saying you want out?' he said quietly. 'Are you saying you want to come back here for good? I thought you loved me, Ellie. I really did.'

Ellie spun onto her knees and looked through the letterbox. He looked so forlorn, so utterly crushed, she could hardly speak. 'I do love you,' she said, in a croaky whisper. He looked round, and her stomach went cold as she saw the sadness in his eyes.

He tried a small smile on for size. 'Good. Come home with me, then.'

Her fingers got tired holding the brass letterbox open and she let it snap shut. Carefully, because she was feeling a bit wobbly, she pulled herself to her feet. He stood too, and leaned against the door, trying to see her through the multi-coloured glass. Ellie raised her fingers to the clear green diamond of glass where she could see his left eye. It reminded her of the colour of the sunset flash. Of true love. Of coming home.

'I'm sorry, Mark. It's just…I just needed to be somewhere that reminded me of Chloe.'

The green eye staring at her through the glass blinked. She knew what he was thinking. He thought she'd come here to remember Sam too. But while she had unearthed forgotten memories of both the people she'd lost, it didn't make the slightest impact on what she felt for Mark.

'I love you, Mark. And as soon as we work out a way to get this door open I'm coming back home. I promise.'

He nodded again, but she could tell he only half believed her. Another wave of emotion hit her and she began to cry again. What was wrong with her today? 'I don't know why I'm doing this,' she said, half-sobbing, half-laughing. 'I can't seem to get a grip...'

'Perhaps it's the hormones?'

Hormones?

She jumped as the brass flap of the letterbox creaked open again. Something plastic rattled through and clattered onto the floor. Her pregnancy test! She'd left it in the sink. So much for a cool, calm testing of the water on that subject.

'When were you going to tell me?' he asked, his voice going cold. 'I didn't expect to find out I'm going to be a father from a plastic stick. You could have called me at the very least.'

'I *was* going to tell you, but then I...I forgot Chloe's name. And that just freaked me out. I was scared. What if I forget her altogether when this new baby comes along? I couldn't live with myself. You do understand, don't you?'

She heard him grumble something under his breath. The heavy crunch of his feet on the gravel got quieter.

'Mark!' Ellie ran to the door and pressed her nose against the glass.

No answer. She'd finally scared him away with

the ghosts from her past. Her unfinished business had caught up with her.

'Mark!' She sounded far too desperate, but she didn't care.

She dropped the test and flung her full weight against the door. Unimpressed, it hardly rattled. She banged it with her fists, hoping to catch Mark's attention. She needed to tell him how stupid she'd been, that she thought he'd be a wonderful father.

'Mark!' Hoarse shouts were punctuated by sobs as she continued to bang on the door.

She stopped.

No faint crunch on the gravel. No hint of a shadow moving up the path. She used the door for support as she slumped against it, exhausted. He couldn't leave now, could he?

She managed one last hollow plea, so quiet he couldn't possibly hear it. 'Don't go.'

'I'm not going anywhere.'

She spun round to find him striding towards her down the hallway.

'How did you—?'

He nodded towards the back door, not slowing until he crushed her close to him. His lips kissed her wet eyelids, her nose, her cheeks, and came to linger on her mouth. She might be confused about many things, but here in his arms everything seemed to make sense. When she finally dragged herself away, she looked into his face. All the passion, tenderness and love she had ever hoped to see there were glistening in his eyes.

'Ellie, there is room in that massive heart of yours for all of us. Easily.' He stroked the side of her face. 'Just because we're going to make new memories together—the three of us—it doesn't mean you have to erase the old ones.'

He dipped his hand into his pocket and pulled something out of it. It was only as she felt cold metal round her neck that she realised he had brought her locket with him, and that he was fastening it at her nape, underneath her hair.

Her lip quivered. 'But what if I *do* forget? My brain's not reliable all the time, is it?'

He looked at her with fierce tenderness. 'You won't forget. I won't let you. If you lose a name or a date I'll remember it for you. We're in this together, Ellie. You and me. And I want all of you. We have the future, but your past has made you who you are now, and that's the woman I love.'

She raised both hands and stroked the sides of his face, looking just as fiercely back at him. 'Oh,

I love you too,' she whispered, and pressed her trembling lips to his.

She had one thing left to ask. Just because she needed to be one hundred percent certain. 'You do want children?'

Waiting for his reaction, she swallowed, trying to ease the thickening in her throat.

His hands moved from her back to splay over her still-flat stomach. She laughed. He looked as if he was expecting evidence there and then. He was just going to have to be patient.

'I want it all. I want our baby. I want to change nappies and clean up sick and crawl around on the floor with him. I want to give him brothers and sisters and teach the whole lot of them to play cricket. I want to help our children with their homework, teach them how to drive, give our daughters away at the altar. And I want to do it all with you by my side. Will you do that with me, Ellie? Do you want that too?'

Ellie threw back her head and laughed with joy. Mark always had made everything seem so simple. She was the one who made it all so complicated. She kissed him with a fervour that surprised them both.

Then, for the second time that month, she said, 'I do.'

EPILOGUE

ELLIE crept across the carpet in her bare feet and peered into the empty cot.

'Shh!' A low voice came from a dim corner of the room. 'I've just got him off to sleep.' Mark was pacing up and down, their two-week-old son cradled against his shoulder.

Baby Miles was sleeping the boneless sleep that newborns did so well. His mouth hung open and his brow was tensed into a frown. Mark and Ellie smiled at each other.

'The trick to putting him into bed is to treat him like a stick of dynamite,' he said, sounding like a total expert already as he lowered the infant into the cot with precision. 'One false move and—'

'The explosion is just as noisy and twice as devastating. I know. You've made that joke a hundred times in the last fortnight, and unfortunately I haven't forgotten a single occasion.'

Mark grinned at her, then went back to what

he'd been doing. He eased his hand from under his son's head. They both froze as the little tyrant stirred and made a squeaky grunt. Mark's mask of stern concentration melted.

'I love it when he makes those noises,' he said, reaching for Ellie's hand and leading her from the room. She lifted their joined hands to look at her watch.

'Midnight! Just the right time for a chocolate feast,' she explained, and pulled him towards the kitchen. She delved into the fridge and pulled out a large bar of her favourite chocolate.

He turned the radio on low, and they ate chocolate and chatted until they were both doing more yawning than munching.

Ellie cocked her head. 'Listen, Mark.' He turned the radio up a notch. It sounded deafening in the quiet kitchen. They both looked at the ceiling and waited. When they were sure it was safe to make a noise, she added, 'They're playing our song.'

He started to hum along to Kat's latest single, 'All My Tomorrows'. It had been number one for three weeks already. The music-buying public couldn't seem to get enough of the simple love song, performed with just the expressive huskiness of Kat's voice and her acoustic guitar.

Ellie smiled and remembered the first time she'd heard it. She could almost feel the warmth of the Carribbean dawn on her skin and smell the hibiscus blossoms. Mark joined in the second chorus. She stood up and ruffled his hair before sitting on his lap. 'Don't give up your day job, sweetie. Kat might have you up on murder charges for doing that to her song.'

Mark pulled a face and Ellie hummed along with the music.

Treasure my heart and keep it safe, and I'll spend all my tomorrows loving you.

Ellie wagged a finger at him. 'Better do as the lady says, Mark.'

'Always,' he said, as he leaned in and stole a kiss.